Remarks from the Judges

"When I sit down with a short story, I'm hoping to be surprised, or unnerved, or waylaid. I want to feel that something is at stake: in the language and structure, in the emotional lives of the characters, in the consequences of their actions. The best stories are almost otherworldly in their dimensions, as if I have opened a small suitcase left on my front door, only to find three geese, a small child, a jewel thief, and her mother emerging. The stories here delighted and surprised and moved me—I'm so very, very glad that I got to read them and that now you do too."

—KELLY LINK, 2017 judge, 2018 MacArthur Fellow,
and author of *Get in Trouble*

"I was really inspired by what I saw here—not just the beautiful weirdness of the writers and their work, but the fact that the stories were published. It made me feel so hopeful."

—CARMEN MARIA MACHADO, 2019 judge and
author of *Her Body and Other Parties*

"It was an honor to read so much exciting debut work for this collection, and I'm thrilled to be a part of introducing these writers' voices to a wider audience. When I love a story, it stops me in my tracks on first read, and makes me want to see what it will do next, and then stays with me to make me pause again days or weeks or years later. The stories in this collection are haunting and compelling in the best ways, full of brilliant voices, striking images, and work that expands our sense of both the capacity of the story form and the capacity of fiction to help us see the world we live in and the futures we might have" —DANIELLE EVANS, 2019 judge and author of *Before Y...*

"There were very well-written stories that didn't end up on the final list, edged out by the magnitude of feeling and creativity contained in the final twelve. I was particularly struck by the authors' ability to hit it out of the park, first time up. When I read I'm always (like it or not) guessing what's going to happen at the end of the line, the scene, on the plot level. The stories we chose were those that forced me, a relentless overthinker, to stop thinking.

"Amy Hempel's first short story was 'In the Cemetery Where Al Jolson Is Buried.' That story is great, and contains many of the elements she's famous for, but it is not like most of her stories. It's way longer, for one, and more traditional. As if she was only able to peel her inhibitions as she wrote more and more. I'm excited for these authors to participate in that same kind of peeling that helps voice grow more substantial, and I hope this honor gives them the confidence to get weirder and weirder, stronger and stronger."

—MARIE-HELENE BERTINO, 2017 judge and
author of *2 A.M. at The Cat's Pajamas* and *Safe as Houses*

"I was so blown away by the pieces we chose for this collection—there was a wonderful array of different styles and approaches in the submissions we received, but each of the stories we ended up choosing had something startlingly alive and bracingly imaginative within it. You can tell that these are writers working with total dedication to gift these fictive worlds to their readers, to make these surprising, vivid scenarios real. I am so wildly enthusiastic about what these writers are going to do next—and in reading this anthology, you get to say you've followed their entire career, from the very first short story on! You can't beat that."

—ALEXANDRA KLEEMAN, 2018 judge and author of
Intimations and *You Too Can Have a Body Like Mine*

"A lot of people talk about how so many short stories are becoming too workshopped, too MFA, too a certain kind of story. And I can say, after reading all the entries here, they are wrong. There are so many stories being told that are extraordinary and unexpected. I fretted over picking only twelve. But the stories that won were all stories that astounded us all." —NINA McCONIGLEY, 2017 judge and author of *Cowboys and East Indians*

Praise for the PEN America Best Debut Short Stories Series

"[An] anthology of remarkable prose . . . The gathered contest winners are uniquely gifted writers whose stories represent literature's bright tomorrow. The pieces showcase a wide breadth of human experiences, representing numerous racial, ethnic, and cultural identities . . . Sharp, engrossing, and sure to leave readers excited about the future of the craft." —*Booklist*

"A great overview of some of the year's most interesting fiction." —*Vol. 1 Brooklyn*

"These are stories that hide behind corners, stories that make grand statements about identity, and stories that offer a full life and times in a small format . . . A strong addition to the annual anthologies." —*PopMatters*

"A greatest hits list for contemporary fiction, a way to quickly get up to speed on what's being published." —*Mental Floss*

"A pleasure for fans of short fiction and a promise of good things to come." —*Kirkus Reviews*

PEN AMERICA BEST DEBUT SHORT STORIES

EDITED BY
YUKA IGARASHI

2019

JUDGES
DANIELLE EVANS
ALICE SOLA KIM
CARMEN MARIA MACHADO

CATAPULT  NEW YORK

Please see Permissions on page 219 for individual credits.

ISBN: 978-1-948226-34-9

Catapult titles are distributed to the trade by Publishers Group West
Phone: 866-400-5351

Printed in the United States of America
10 9 8 7 6 5 4 3 2 1

CONTENTS

INTRODUCTION

I CAN THINK of different ways to introduce you to the stories in this collection—twelve chosen for the Dau Prize, out of hundreds nominated, by Danielle Evans, Alice Sola Kim, and Carmen Maria Machado, all by writers who had never published fiction before 2018. I could describe the interesting things that happen in them: a "good black girl" climbs the flagpole in front of the capitol building in South Carolina to take down its Confederate flag; a woodcutter loses his way home and meets a man wearing a mask made from a taxidermied wolf. I could focus on the playful and daring stylistic choices—one is written in the form of panels for a manga, and another includes incantatory poems and fragments from Audre Lorde and Sun Tzu. I could discuss the ways they engage with "issues" I care about, such as postpartum depression, sexual violence, immigration, mass incarceration, and rural poverty. I could try to explain why the stories set in seventeenth-century France and in Beijing after Mao Zedong's death and during a tornado on an Oklahoma farm in 1956 seem as current as the stories that take place in the present, how every one of them feels to me as though they could only have been written today.

While all this might encourage you to read what follows—I hope it does—I find myself wanting to be more specific. I want to get you closer to how I experienced these stories. What moves me when I read, what I remember best, tends to be smaller than plot, structure, theme, or setting. It's often a sentence or a detail. Or it's more elusive. Here are a dozen moments, one from each piece, when something rose up from the page and entered my mind to become a feeling.

• In "Today, You're a Black Revolutionary" by Jade Jones, when the narrator finds herself at the top of that Confederate-flag-bearing pole:

> How many different people control you? The flag is rough and
> flaps wildly in your grip. You thought it would be made of bet-
> ter material. Silk or satin or something.
>   "Ma'am!" a gruff voice shouts below. "Come down, now!"
>   "In a moment," you answer.

What a funny, polite thing to say while engaged in the most re-bellious act of one's life; how fitting that one would contemplate the texture of a piece of fabric while confronting the country's history of racial oppression.

• From "The Rickies" by Sarah Curry, told in the collective voice of four women who meet at a campus potluck for rape victims and become friends when they're the only ones to call bullshit on "survival":

> That semester after study abroad, freshmen girls with Bibles
> in hand-knit cozies were the worst. Anytime they saw a girl
> alone on campus, they invited her to Bible study: *Free soda!*
> *Hot Christian guys!* We patted their heads. They were wide-
> eyed Yorkies in a puppy mill and didn't know it. We said,

Sorry, we are atheists of everything. But it troubled us. Atheists sounded too positive. Nihilists was too descriptive. All -ists too reductive.

There are so many layers packed into this passage: the pain and disillusionment behind the words "after study abroad" (and the shock of recognizing what happens to many women during their college summer travels); the sense of superiority toward freshmen that quickly gives way to uncertainty and unease; the women's refusal to be part of any group, as victims or as anything else, in contrast to the obvious solidarity they feel with one another.

- The transporting opening lines of Kelsey Peterson's "The Unsent Letters of Blaise and Jacqueline Pascal," which immediately changes my perception of nature, math, shapes, and the universe:

  I saw a perfect circle today. The yellow disk at the center of an anemone bloomed early and whose white petals had curled back in the wind. I marveled at its humble perfection, springing forth from some superabundance of the unrelenting spring. I am curious if there is an equation for such a flower, the formula to project its arcs and angles, its radii and planes.

- The ending to "The Manga Artist" by Doug Henderson, in which a drawing of a mouse and a hamster encapsulates all the complexity of the human love story that precedes it:

Panel 115: Alfonso and Hamuchan have left the school. They are running down the wide front stairs, fear and excitement in their eyes.

- A portrait of a marriage in three sentences, from Laura Freudig's "Mother and Child":

John is tall enough to stand behind me and rest his chin on my head. He likes to do this. I do not know how I feel about it: cherished or pinned down.

- In "Without a Big One" by JP Infante, about a boy and his slippery relationships with the adults around him—his mother, Mary; his absent stepfather; and his beautiful babysitter:

That morning you realize the Chinese doctor was flirting with [Mary]. You make a mental note to tell your stepfather when he calls from school. He's only called a couple of times since he left because the apartment phone is always being cut off and there are never minutes on Mary's prepaid cell phone.

Your babysitter, Nilda, calls you Ray Ray . . . Nilda is taller than Mary and has a fat ass. Whenever you hug her, you touch it and she doesn't say anything. Nilda is in love with you. You don't tell her you know because she has a boyfriend.

These paragraphs remind me that growing up often seems like an initiation into secrets—not just learning them, but understanding which ones to share and which ones to keep.

- A few words in Tamiko Beyer's "Last Days 1" that create an entirely new world:

  > There were five of us in that small apartment, hauling water, coding and decoding, soldering metal, constructing strategies, drafting poems. I lifted heavy objects and learned to stitch up an open wound.

- In "Good Hope" by Enyeribe Ibegwam, as the narrator arrives at a building in Washington, D.C., to see a favorite uncle for the first time since he left Nigeria decades before:

  > A teenage girl with flowing multicolor hair, wearing black harem trousers and a yellow top that bared her midriff, raced up the stairs behind me and stopped to flash me a letter. Before I could look at it, she screamed, "I got accepted," and continued past me, tears slick on her brown face.

  The girl never appears again; she's a splash of color that illuminates the uncle's home in a way that a straightforward description of it never could.

- From "Tornado Season" by Melinda Manalokas, a portrayal of sex that seems especially powerful and unexpected for being from the point of view of a fourteen-year-old farm girl in the 1950s:

  > The first time he asked her to be on top, she was embarrassed at first, but then something else happened, a connection made

between being with him and the way she would rub herself against her bed at night. She started concentrating, gathering the threads of it, and then there it was—dizzying, boundless, like air or water or light.

- It's better if I don't explain why this exchange in Pingmei Lan's "Cicadas and the Dead Chairman" delights me so much; it's part of a theme that quietly recurs and gathers meaning as the story progresses:

  "What's your name, little girl?" The driver looked at me through his rearview mirror.

  "Shut up," I said.

- I could pick almost any section in A. B. Young's "Vain Beasts," whose interweaving of ancient motifs reminds me of a fugue:

  The wolf tells the woodcutter, "In exchange for stealing my rose, you will bring me your most beautiful possession."

  The woodcutter trembles. He wishes he had not left his axe back among the tree stumps. He could split the wolf into equal halves, had he enough force behind his swing.

  The wolf says, "My vanity makes me patient, woodcutter. I have waited many years for beauty."

  The woodcutter lies through his sharp teeth. "I have no beautiful possessions. I am a poor woodcutter."

  "What?" says the wolf. "No wife? No daughter?"

- Finally, in "Bad Northern Women" by Erin Singer, a paragraph I've thought about many times since I first read it, in which the narrators seem to break through the story's walls to address the reader directly, demanding to be acknowledged:

> Before we die we'll slick your Teen Burgers with Teen sauce, make chicken salad on a cheese bun and keep your kids from drowning in the public pool and we are jolly bun fillers of submarine sandwiches and we ring up your Trojans and Lysol and scented candles, and we shovel your snow and push your babies on the swing set, pare your grandpa's toenails, harvest your honey, detail your urinals, hold the papery hands of your dying, nestle newspapers in the rungs of your mailbox and ladle gravy on your French fries and we push logs through your sawmill, bring you size-ten Sorels, then size eleven, then size ten and a half, and climb onto our mattresses at night with gasoline on our hands and dog bites on our ankles, chicken fingers on our breath, cigarette smoke in our hair, ringing in our ears and our men's hands snaking up our thighs.

A list like this will probably mean more to you once you've read the book. The extracts here aren't meant to represent the stories, because of course one passage can't represent a story, whose effect is always cumulative. And of course every reader's list will be different; my own list might be different on a different day. The list only represents the possibility of infinite lists like this—infinite moments within these pages by which we might find our way to an infinite variety of emotions.

THIS ANTHOLOGY IS in its third year. Its previous contributors have signed with agents, published stories and books, inspired other writers. Compared to other annual best-of collections, though, it's still young. The first volume of *Best American Short Stories* came out in 1915; *The O. Henry Prize Stories* started in 1919; *The Pushcart Prize* is a little over forty years old. As with those prizes and series, I think the influence of this prize and series on its winners, and the influence of its winners on literature, will only become clearer as years and decades pass.

For now, I want to make two observations. There are a handful of magazines that have impressed our judges each year with the debut writers they've discovered. *The Rumpus* has had a piece in every edition; *Black Warrior Review, Epiphany, The Baltimore Review*, and *Conjunctions* have all contributed multiple stories. It seems to me that anyone interested in the future of short stories would want to pay special attention to these publications. I've come to think of them—and all twenty-nine magazines that have appeared in these anthologies—as bright places in the "literary landscape" that I'm glad to know and glad I get to visit. To further push this metaphor, the editors of the magazines who originally published these stories, and whose expert commentaries introduce each piece, are the innkeepers and hosts, hanging their welcoming lights; the judges are the explorers who find and forge paths to them.

The other observation is about pleasure. Sometimes when I'm talking about contemporary writing, I hear—and find myself using—words like "necessary" or "urgent." This may doubly be true of short stories, which have been seen as necessary not just for readers but for writers as well, a kind of career stepping-stone. Often anthologies also address a need or fill a lack. This particular one arose because the Dau family, PEN America, and Catapult found there was nothing else like it, no book that showcased fiction by debut writers. It's supposed to serve as motivation to read and publish unfamiliar names; it's a yearly argument for risk and novelty. I do think these stories, and this series, offer something that no other writing does. And yet I feel the need to insist that you don't need to read them. Nobody needs to write, or read, any story. But then what a joy—a triumph, a small miracle—that we can.

YUKA IGARASHI
Series Editor

PEN AMERICA BEST DEBUT SHORT STORIES 2019

EDITOR'S NOTE

The Rumpus works to be a home for stories that build bridges, tear down walls, and speak truth to power. Jade Jones's "Today, You're a Black Revolutionary" accomplishes all of these goals. Jones is completely in control of her craft, utilizing the second-person point of view to draw readers in and offer us full access to the narrator's perspective. And while Jones's narrator is in many ways a hero, she is also a flawed character whose humanity makes it that much easier to establish ourselves within her world.

We believe Jade Jones's artful, timely story is precisely the kind of first publication the PEN/Robert J. Dau Short Story Prize is meant to reward, and we couldn't be prouder that Jade Jones and her writing have been celebrated this year.

Marisa Siegel, Editor in Chief
The Rumpus

TODAY, YOU'RE A BLACK REVOLUTIONARY

Jade Jones

YOU WALK BY the flag twice every day. Once on your way to work and once on your way back home. You've only recently noticed that it affects your mood. It can be perfectly sunny, just the right amount of breeze to cool your skin and not to sweat out your edges. But there it is. The worst part is, it looks majestic, crinkled in the wind. The confident, aggressive contrast of the blue X on the red background. A color combination that says, "Fuck you and your eyes." It rebels against the idea of pleasurable aesthetics. You've noticed that after seeing the flag, you're irritable and easily annoyed by strangers on the bus. A blond child incessantly telling knock-knock jokes to her mother—something you would usually laugh about—is just another example of how frustrating the world can be. You keep your grumpy thoughts to yourself. The world, especially this little blond jester, doesn't deserve all your hate. Does it? Usually, you forget about it by the time you sit down at your desk. Someone else does something more distracting. Today, Wendy the Manager calls you "articulate," and even though you cringe, you don't say anything. The good intentions coat the racism like the casing of a pill. You stay silent and swallow the discomfort. Let it go. Again.

ON YOUR WAY home, you wear your headphones. It's hard to be angry about anything when the outside world is muted. But, today, your post-work soundtrack is interrupted by the carefree yells of children.

The annual end-of-summer fair takes place in the capitol building's plaza. Booths sell fried chicken and bedazzled PROUD TO BE SOUTH CAROLINIAN T-shirts. You try to walk quickly and go unnoticed. These events are for families and knickknack lovers. Your mom, bougie as ever, calls fairs and carnivals "germ pits." Since you've moved to South Carolina last month, you've counted at least one county event each week. People are proud to live here in a way you've never experienced. You haven't heard anyone use the word "stuck" yet.

A group of children spray each other with Super Soakers. They are different shades of brown like the assortment of candies in a box of chocolates. You take your headphones off. Sometimes you cut yourself off from the world.

"That's how you miss the beauty of life," your mom always said when you used to take your headphones everywhere in high school. She can be poetic. She still finds time to paint and send you handmade cards praising you for not going to that MFA program.

"Gotchu!" A tall boy squirts a shorter boy.

"Imma kill you." The boy, whose entire front is wet, laughs. "Get him!"

The three other boys give chase. They run in a circle, and you laugh as you navigate through their game. This is how you would

have normally felt about the child on the bus if you weren't being such a grump. Consumed by the innocence and optimism only
expressed by children and yellow labs. Excited about the future
because, for these beautiful children, the world is open to anything.

You say, "Excuse me," but they don't seem capable of stop-
ping. Good. You don't want them to stop. They're having too much
fun. One boy does say, "Excuse me, ma'am," before he almost runs
over your feet. You could live in this moment.

"When I get you," the boy with the wet shirt huffs, "Imma
beat you like Emmett Till!" He's still smiling while he runs. You
stop abruptly, and one of the boys has to brake with his heels to
avoid colliding into you. It doesn't seem fair to blame Lil Wayne
and his lyrics. Do they know who Emmett Till was? Do they have
an image of his battered face, his features beaten into smudges?
Or is he just another mythical childhood threat, a boogieman,
Bloody Mary? The children are still laughing, effortlessly dodging
in and out of the crowd. The fair attendees bargain over the price
of necklaces and scarves. You stand dumbfounded, and the boys
run farther down the plaza to an area where adults won't get in
the way.

The children are okay. All four of them, now wet and glimmer-
ing in the sun, yell and threaten each other gleefully. Above them,
the flag bats in the wind. Who do you blame for this moment? Lil
Wayne, painfully overt symbolism, your touchy sentimentality?

The flag blows on the pole like it belongs there. It looks as bright
and natural in front of the capitol building as the sun looks in the
sky. It does not look like it has been there for only forty years. It
looks historic and permanent. Questioning it would be like someone tilting their head up to the sky and challenging the placement of
the stars. You put your headphones back in and go home.

———

LATER, YOU CALL him to complain. Now that you're broken up, midnight is too late to call, but you have spent the last few hours thinking about the kids and the flag by yourself. You looked up natural hair tutorials on YouTube but somehow ended up watching Stokely Carmichael clips and finishing *The Black Power Mixtape*.

"Why are you calling?" he whispers. He answered, though, and that means something.

"Something really got to me today," you slur theatrically. No, this is not your first time doing this. The first time you made this mistake, you panicked and thought of a way to make the decision to call him seem less shameful. It's now your schtick.

"Christ," he says, "you're drunk, again?" You're not drunk. You're only pretending to be. He stays on the phone longer when he thinks you're drunk. Missing him is not a good enough reason to call. Drunk means you can take it back. No accountability. It's cliché and cheap, but you're not above any of that. In ten years, you'll use the excuse "I was so young and dumb in my twenties."

You want to talk about the kids, the flag, the injustice and cruelty of the world. No one else really talks about that stuff with you. But the conversation doesn't go that way. The man you thought you were going to love tells you you're an alcoholic. Get help. Not because he loves you or because he is worried, but because your drunk calls are getting old. You keep waking up his new girl. Yeah, the light-skinned trick with the eyelashes in his profile picture.

"Trust me on this," he says. His Beyoncé look-alike is asleep next to him. "You need help."

You were never able to trust him even when trusting him was the thing you wanted most in the world. Even when you were searching for reasons to trust him, sifting through your memories for any small glimmer that this man—despite his own words—was the right person to trust. Remember when he got you coffee that one time you were hungover (maybe you do drink too much) or when he said something about meeting your mother? Isn't that how trustworthy people act?

You need help. Not even you can pretend the man ever cared about your needs.

"Okay," you say.

Fuck him, you decide. And everyone else.

THE IMPORTANT THING to remember when climbing a pole, a rope, a mountain is to not look down. It is classic elementary gym teacher advice, but it still holds true. Shimmy the red strap up, then the black strap. Right foot, left foot. You repeat and to your amazement (and the amazement of the growing crowd around you), you're really climbing this pole.

"I can do all things through Christ," you pray. You're a Christian during bad airplane turbulence and, apparently, when you're climbing poles. It is only when you're halfway up that you start to fear that you aren't doing any of this for yourself. What if it's just a "fuck you" to your mom and the Dark and Lovely relaxer set she sent you for Christmas? Or a theatrical attempt to show him that your world can be bigger than just him? Or perhaps you're here because the jolly mall Santa Claus of a cashier said, "Be careful using this, little lady," when you rented the climbing kit. How many different people control you? The flag is rough and flaps wildly in your grip. You thought it would be made of better material. Silk or satin or something.

"Ma'am!" a gruff voice shouts below. "Come down, now!"

"In a moment," you answer.

How did a bundle of synthetic thread ever make you feel so powerless? At the top of the pole, you are now the banner, the pride of the state.

"Ma'am!"

You wave the flag in the air to a smattering of applause.

"Yes, sista," a woman says with the type of warmth and camaraderie usually reserved for church. You right-foot-left-foot slide until you reach the ground.

You're another blip on the arrest report. The holding cell is a lackluster sea-foam green, and you stare at the concrete for twenty minutes before someone comes to speak to you. You are ready to fight the power, channel Soul Mother Davis, but you don't have to.

"A bottle of water?" the guard asks.

"No, thank you."

They don't press charges, and the guard even mumbles a lukewarm "Take care" when you walk out with your climbing equipment bundled in your arms. The flag is back up by the time you walk home.

They call you a revolutionary. Someone else on the news calls you a troublemaker. You stop watching the news. He calls. He says you looked brave up there on that pole with the flag in your hands. You ask him where Beyoncé is, and he is quiet. Even though you don't want to, you apologize. You never liked people being mad at you. You blame society for that. He asks how you are, and you say "good" with a little too much enthusiasm for it to sound natural.

"Oh," he says. He sounds surprised. "Good."

You lean back against your pillows. Being on the phone with him, you in your pajamas, him probably wearing those nylon basketball shorts, feels familiar. The feeling you get when you return to your apartment after work or when you get a care package from your mother. A blanket of relief. The universe still cares enough to create happy moments for you.

"I should've never let you go," he says. You are not young and dumb enough that you don't recognize the trap, but you are not old and wise enough to snub it. You want to be the woman who says she didn't play into his games. That he tried to come back to you only to discover you were never waiting. But yesterday you went to the Whole Foods to read a book just because you missed the sound of people talking over plates of food. The couple next to you was arguing with their teenage son about his phone bill. The mother groaning between bites, the father huffing. Even the sound of the teenager sucking his teeth had a nice ring to it. You didn't even get through chapter 1 because you had to hear how the argument ended. Yes, he is familiar, but the Whole Foods strangers made you feel a combination of familiar and happy. Comfortable.

"Hello?" he says.

"I'm seeing someone," you say. You're a liar, but at least you're the type of woman Lauryn Hill sings about.

"Really?" He sounds more surprised than angry. Angry would have been good. Angry would have made something in you flutter. But surprise is just insulting.

You have practiced this moment. When you enact your revenge with the most eviscerating, verbal uppercut of the century. To the misfortune of your coworkers, you have practiced this at your desk. Sometimes you get carried away and say "not uh" to the responses you imagine he will say. You'll tell him how shittily he treated you. How you felt like a side chick. Lower than a side chick. A one-night stand that you forget about until you see them at a singles' bar two years later. That is how you felt with him. You'll tell him about his communication issues and the suffocating ideas of toxic masculinity he inherited from his no-good father. You'll make sure you say the part you rehearsed the most: his inability to be vulnerable will leave him empty for the rest of his life. You'll sound like a robot, but a kick-ass feminist robot.

You suck your teeth. "What do you mean *really*?" You notice how you sound like your mother and every other black woman ever. You embrace the stereotypical sass because you feel powerful. "You must not know 'bout me." He used to laugh when you worked song lyrics into your conversations. "You were the problem."

There is the silence that always follows a mic-drop moment. You are about to start the spiel (no-good father, side chick, inability to . . .) when he says, "See, that's your problem." The power is shifting away from you, but you cannot think of how to get it back. It is already too late. "You think you're rare or something."

It feels like whatever has been keeping your brain in its place is now pushing against it. There is a hand on either side of your brain, squeezing it. This is what it always comes down to: your pride or him.

"Turn on your TV and tell me I'm not," you say. Bam. You hang up the phone because courage like that is fleeting. You *almost* cry. You tell yourself that it is more important that it looked like a victory than felt like a victory.

Your mom calls and responds to your greeting with a sigh. "You know med school faculty own televisions, don't you?"

You tell her you'll call her back later.

"Tomorrow," she says. "I don't have nothing else to say to you tonight."

The reporters start to call the same night. You only answer questions from the liberal news outlets. One of them asks, "How did you become such a strong woman?" You're not supposed to be insulted by that.

"What, you mean physically?" you say.

You do three more interviews like that. One of them asks you to do a live interview for the local morning show. They love your story, the woman on the phone says twice.

"Sure, why not," you say. It was not the response she was expecting. You smile to make her feel more comfortable, but then you remember you're on the phone. "I'd love to," you add.

You're pretty sure you hear her sigh, relieved. "Great, we can't wait to meet you," she says.

FOR THE SHOW, you wear a black dress and a red scarf. The woman left a message last night saying not to be nervous. Just dress and act like the "authentic you," she'd said. She seems surprised when she meets you, but she pulls it together quickly. She's a professional.

"The red-and-black contrast may be a bit too harsh for the cameras. It doesn't really match our set," she says. You hesitate but ultimately take off the scarf.

During the interview, you are sitting in a leather chair that makes uncomfortable sounds when you move. The woman sits across from you. The set looks like the living rooms you always admire in Pottery Barn. There is even a bookcase. With books. Fake books, you surmise bitterly.

The interview is about to start. She says don't be nervous. You say you're not. Why aren't you nervous? She asks about you. You tell her about yourself: age, schooling, how well you get along with your mom.

"No, no," she says. "Tell us about the real you," she says.

You try not to look unnerved. Who does she think you were just talking about?

"I don't understand," you say, and you curse yourself and live TV. You'd do anything for a retake.

She is a natural. She's loving this. "Well, we talked to some of your friends and family, and so many people said the same thing. They were shocked!" Her emphasis and joy on the last word are Oprahtic. They almost knock you over like a gust of wind. "The good girl. Ivy League educated, med-school bound. No one suspected you to climb on a pole and take the flag like a rebel." The image of you on a pole annoys you when she says it, but not as much as the image of you as a rebel. Isn't her job to choose words carefully?

"I don't know," you say, and she is less charmed by your confusion this time. She waits for an answer. "I guess the people you talked to don't know me very well."

"This is just a very bold move for someone with your pedigree. Threats have been made against your life," she says. You know this. You made sure not to Google yourself, but you couldn't ignore the phone calls, deep breathing, and hang-ups. The first time it happened last night, you answered the phone without looking because you thought it was him. "Your acquaintances said you never seemed like the rebel type."

She smiles for her audience. Not for you. She is growing impatient with you. This was a setup. You are being played as the good-black-girl-turned-rebel. They want the black Avril Lavigne, the suburban Nat Turner.

Why are you misbehaving? she wants to ask. We want to watch you misbehave and record the story, but why?

Why are you being this way with this woman? You agreed to this interview. You took off the red scarf and smiled into that camera. You will be thought of as the rebellious twenty-something who tore down the flag like a teenager who, frustrated with her parents, gets the red highlights anyway. You want to say: I'm tired of being reminded every day that people in this world hate me. That people want me dead. Felt strongly enough to fight and die in a war because they hated me that much. That they raised kids to hate and that even if their great-great-grandkids can't admit it, sometimes they hate me, too. I want to walk to work and think about something dumb like my new Post-it Notes or that email I don't want to send. I can't be mad every morning anymore.

All of that would be political, a word you know has somehow developed a poisonous connotation. You shouldn't say any of that, should you?

"The flag is back up," you say instead.

"Yes," she says. She waits.

"I'm going to take it down. They're going to keep putting it back up, and I'm going to keep taking it back down," you say.

She looks at you with the spread smile and alarmed eyes of someone talking to a person who they just realized is crazy. "Okay," she says, "but groups like the KKK are saying they are going to guard the flag at all costs. And you are—not to dismiss you in any way—just one twenty-something. Are you scared?"

You lean back into the chair, a gesture that adds a dramatic effect you did not intend. "I'm done being scared," you say. "You tell
the Klan all the scared niggers are dead."

She is colorless, as if someone has vacuumed all of the red from
her cheeks. "Oh my god," she says, seemingly without even real-
izing it. Someone is gesturing wildly in the corner. Commercial
break, they mouth. "I—we have to—thank you for joining us, and
after the break, sports with Larry Potowski."

She doesn't look at you at first. She folds her hands in her lap.
"I'm going to have to ask you to leave," she says. When you don't
move, she looks at you. "Leave now, please." Her tone is painfully
professional, the way you imagine she talks to her cleaning lady.
The security guard moves slowly toward the set. You leave.

OUTSIDE, YOU SEE your mom is calling you. You told her to wake
up early and watch the show. When you ignore it, she calls again.
You ignore it. Now she'll have two lectures prepared the next time
she talks to you.

You take another way home, so you don't have to walk by the
capitol building. You listen to your mom's voice mails. You count
the word "crazy" eight times. She asks, too earnestly, if you're on
drugs. There is a text message from him. The preview on your lock
screen says, "Holy shit . . ." He still thinks you're friends. You
won't text him back.

You enter your apartment and the sun coming through the
blinds is almost too bright. You took off work for the interview,
and it's rare that you get to be in your apartment in the height of
the morning. You sit on your couch with a book. All the scared

niggers are dead, you think to yourself and laugh. You have never liked yourself more.

―――――――――――

Jade Jones was born and raised in southern New Jersey. A former Kimbilio Fiction Fellow, she is a graduate of Princeton University and the Iowa Writers' Workshop, where she was a Teaching-Writing Fellow. She is currently a lecturer in Writing Arts at Rowan University, where she teaches first-year writing and creative writing.

EDITOR'S NOTE

As soon as we read the first lines of "The Rickies," we knew that we had something special on our hands. Sarah Curry's movement of you/me/we in these opening paragraphs dug immediately into the heart of this story, a tale of four young women who have all survived sexual violence and their singular and communal ways of coping with their assaults. "The Rickies" is brutally honest in illustrating its characters' emotions and complexity. As Curry writes, the Rickies are "the bravest and worst parts" of these young women at the same time. It is not a story with a happy ending; in fact, it eschews a solid resolution to focus on the fact that the Rickies' personal stories are still unfolding, are still changing.

That this story came to us at the height of the #MeToo movement was not the reason we chose it, but it did serve to emphasize the universality of the experiences portrayed here—and also the grace with which Curry depicted them. We selected and published "The Rickies" as a finalist for *Nimrod*'s Francine Ringold Awards for New Writers, which celebrate the work of new writers with original, distinct voices, writers who are just beginning to publish their work but who we are sure will go on to achieve greater literary success and share many more unique stories with the world. "The Rickies" was a perfect example of this kind of story.

Eilis O'Neal, Editor in Chief
Nimrod International Journal

THE RICKIES

Sarah Curry

You didn't know me then.

We were all girls, about the same size, no more than 5'3" and under 115 pounds, but that fall back on campus from study abroad we walked like we were men, nearly 6'1" and 200 pounds with a bum knee. Arms flexed and at our sides. We wanted to look like a stuffed gorilla won at a carnival by slinging little wooden balls as hard as you can at glass milk bottles. We walked as though we had sledgehammers affixed to our shoulders, and our names were Ricky.

Why Ricky?

You know, Ricky the mechanic. Ricky the prizefighter (or was that Rocky?). Ricky the uncle who belches the alphabet.

It was a joke. Sort of.

We met at a "survivors" group potluck where a bunch of female college students took dainty nervous bites of cupcakes and later cried as they told their stories. Except us. One after the other we left as a circle massage started to form, pretending we had to pee or had an emergency text. We met outside and called bullshit on "survival." We didn't even exchange names. We headed to the closest apartment and drank ourselves silly. Or should I say serious?

The next morning we shed our flowing travelers' skirts, our

spaghetti-strap tank tops, our black ExOfficio bikini-cut underwear. One of us burned them. I can't remember who. Someone else
stuffed them in a Goodwill bin, and another cut them with kitchen
scissors and threw them in the trash. I kept mine, shoving them
deep into the box under my bed.

We put on jeans and ironic T-shirts. We tied bandanas over our
hair. See here, I still have them: yellow, purple, red, and turquoise.
Sometimes, I tie one around Chloe, my dog, an Australian shepherd. But I always remember to put them back in the box and shut
it tight.

We dropped out of belly-dancing club and yoga and admitted
we didn't care that much about saving Darfur (though I did stay on
their email list. I don't know about the others). We went to the same
corner of the cafeteria as the vegetarian meet-up and chewed on
chicken legs and took big bites of Salisbury steak with our mouths
open.

At Kroger, we spied a Delta Zeta limping under the weight of
three six-packs of hard lemonade, and we scowled. We professed a
preference for bourbon. Bulleit. Because we liked staring into the
bartender's eyes and asking for it straight, the way he scratched his
biceps uncomfortably as if he were trying to dig birdshot out from
under his skin. We liked that—making others uncomfortable.

In October, we got tattoos that said "Mom," and when they
healed we used Sharpies to add "Never a," "Hate," and "Blame."
Why was it our mothers' faults? We couldn't say exactly, but we
knew we never wanted to be one. We vowed especially never to have
daughters and, most of all, never to name them Lisa, Annabelle,
Beth, or Claire.

In November, we started going to the gun range for Ladies'
Night. There was an acrid smell in the air. At the range, we willed

our arms to become part of the weapon and hurl pieces of metal through a paper target shaped like the outline of a man's hyperbolic death throe. There's a factory in Billings, Montana, that produces reams of these on recycled paper—neon green, pink, and black; the groin, heart, and head all "ultra-scale." We kept the factory up and running. I still do. Each round released short hollow yips that echoed into one long scream, if we pulled the trigger fast enough.

That semester after study abroad, freshmen girls with Bibles in hand-knit cozies were the worst. Anytime they saw a girl alone on campus, they invited her to Bible study: *Free soda! Hot Christian guys!* We patted their heads. They were wide-eyed Yorkies in a puppy mill and didn't know it. We said, Sorry, we are atheists of everything. But it troubled us. Atheists sounded too positive. Nihilists was too descriptive. All -ists too reductive.

We were the Rickies.

It took weeks to lose the brown skin of summer and whiten, but by November we were the color of turned milk. People stopped asking where we'd gone, if we'd had fun, if they should *ohmygod go on study abroad next year.* To be clear, after our summers in different *to-die-for* locales, we no longer believed in the mysticism of Chichen Itza, Stonehenge, Chiang Mai, or Kathmandu, or in men named Sergio, Gavin, Sonthi, or Yash.

We tried to remember and then not remember the faces of our rapists so many times and for so long that they blurred and merged. Their faces were nondescript and smooth as mannequins, as burn victims growing new skin, faces that could be anyone.

So we avoided everyone.

Not one of us had a picture of her rapist, so don't look for them in the box. We searched the corners of selfies and pictures of

impromptu street scenes, but they weren't there. There was one picture on my phone (dead now, of course, and in the box) of my hand
holding a piece of yellow street corn charred at the edges. There is
a long shadow cast over the shot. Is that the vendor or Sergio? Or
is it me?

What is in the box? Belle's ticket stub from her night bus ride
from Chiang Mai to Bangkok; a bar napkin Claire found in her
purse the morning after she woke up puking and confused in a
hostel bed that wasn't hers; and the Gore-Tex raincoat of the expat
who date-raped Beth in her sleeping bag in her backpacking tent
on the third day of her ten-day trek through the Himalayas. The
semester we met her, we got used to the heat of Beth's apartment.
She would crank up the space heater so she could sleep without
bedding. No matter a blanket's texture, she hated its roughness,
its weight on her skin at night. It didn't matter how cold it grew
outside; we sweated at Beth's.

That Christmas break, as presents to one another, we went to
the courthouse and stood in line with applications to change our
names.

Because like Madonna or Cher we would have no last names,
we each decided to spell it differently. Belle called dibs on Ricky
because it was her idea. She was weird and smart and always went a
little too far. Claire pouted and then chose Rickey. She complained
that she didn't like how innocent it looked, but Claire looked like a
serious sweet girl painted by a Dutch artist. It fit her. Beth said she
thought she would be more hopeful with a name that ended in "i."
She helps troubled kids climb mountains now. I'd say Ricki worked
for her. I didn't know who I wanted to be, but Rickie seemed dull.
I hoped Rici might look kind of cosmopolitan. Everyone asked me
how to pronounce it.

We filled out the paperwork, but they wouldn't accept it or take our hundred dollars each until we put a notice in the newspaper for a week.

"Like a paper newspaper?" we asked. We thought the news only existed online.

The bemused clerk was irritating but helpful. "Yes. You know how when someone gets married the public gets to object? Same thing. You might be taking someone's uncle's name. All of you." His eyebrows wriggled up and down with silent laughter.

We turned away.

We found newspapers in a box outside the courthouse that took only coins, which we borrowed from a woman standing at a bus stop. We touched the newspaper's dry thin pages. Ink rubbed off on our hands. We said, "Do you remember?" But we didn't finish, because the smell reminded us of our fathers and eating breakfast cereal in grade school and how mornings used to smell like Cheerios and ink and all of a sudden we wanted that. We wanted our fathers and Cheerios. But we weren't going to get it, so we called to place a notice. We pictured rubber-banded pages tossed onto doorsteps in the freezing dark blue of morning.

A few days later, in ten-point type on the last page of the local section, our notices, one each, were listed. Somewhere, people who still woke up at 7 a.m. read about us. We did not know anyone who woke up at 7 a.m. Not even people with 8 a.m. classes. We pictured ourselves as cowboys at dawn at the town's breakfast table. We waited for gunslingers.

But all that came was the mail. See here the notices, which my mother cut from the newspaper and placed in this envelope and mailed to my apartment with no note. None of the other mothers lived in town.

Still, when no texts were sent, no flight itineraries emailed, two mothers called to ask when their daughters would be home for Christmas. They were sent to voice mail. *Working on my senior thesis over break*, Ricky texted. *Ski trip with friends!! Barely a signal!* wrote Ricki. The third mother did not call. She was on a cruise.

And so legally we became the Rickies.

We spent most of December and January in our apartments. We curled up on the radiators, drinking saucers of black coffee, looking out at the snow.

Then it happened. In February of all months, Rickey and Ricki fell in love. With each other.

"This is bullshit," we (halved) said. "Love doesn't exist."

"We believe love might exist. Especially if it's between Rickies. Besides, you know we've always liked girls." They laced fingers and called each other Ricky-baby.

"That's not your name," we (halved) reminded them.

That week they did not invite us to meet them for $2 hamburger night, but we saw them there anyway. It was awkward. They talked about old films we'd never heard of. A few weeks later they moved in together. And then, inevitably, they bought a kitten.

They invited us over to meet the kitten. We made fun of the invitation but went anyway. Their apartment smelled of curry and clove cigarettes. Rickey heated up a pan in their coat closet of a kitchen. She swirled broth and tomatoes with chickpeas and potatoes.

"Rici, will you toss me the garam masala?" She pointed to a shoebox of spices under their futon.

Ricki sat on the floor smoking and waving a piece of yarn for the kitten. "We don't eat meat anymore. You guys should definitely try it. Seriously, every time we eat chickpeas or roasted Brussels sprouts it's like insta-Popeye. You feel so powerful."

We looked around. They had traded coffee for tins of green tea. We spied jogging shoes by the door. And there was the kitten.

"You mean spinach," we said.

They looked at us blankly.

"Popeye eats spinach."

"Oh, right. Well, he should have eaten kale. It's a superfood."

We stared at the teensy cat asleep on Ricki's lap, tired from batting its small pink paws at things. Its name was Mittens, if you can believe it. We couldn't.

Here is a teeny tiny shed claw from Mittens that I dug out of their rug and put in my jeans pocket. Is that weird? I liked running my finger against it to feel its little bite.

"So, what will you do with the cat when you break up?" Ricky asked.

We went weeks without seeing them.

THAT SPRING, OUR last before graduation, we headed to class through a gauntlet of bodies. The quad was littered with girls in shorts and bikinis and boys tossing Frisbees. We stared straight ahead, sweating through our thrift-store sweaters. We saw Rickey and Ricki on a picnic blanket. We stood there while they discussed cheap flights to Morocco. Rickey mentioned a summer internship. They ate fresh fruit. Pear juice dribbled down their chins.

We wanted so badly to feel the sun on our skin, to lick off the sweetness.

Here is the pear sticker that Ricki playfully stuck to my cheek that I moved to my scratchy sweater, which I never wore again. In the box, all my clumpy sweaters from that time tangle together, a woolen nest to give rest to other ugly things.

That night, the pear night, the two of us (the remaining Rickies) watched a movie about two girl lawyers who—surprise—fall in love. We sat shoulder to shoulder, the laptop askew as it balanced on our legs. Its warmth heated our thighs. We shimmied out of our jeans and crawled into bed. We wrapped our legs around each other and kissed. We kissed again. We swirled our tongues into each other's mouth, hoping for some sweetness, like two halves of a McDonald's soft-serve joining on a cone.

Our grinding was effortful. As though we were taking some standardized test that we might pass if we could better darken the circles. We pushed our pencils down into the wood desk until the tips broke and the page tore through. We could not erase the summer. We just left streaks across a page.

We did not fall in love, get cute haircuts, go somewhere sunny, or become girl lawyers in dashing pantsuits, defending the undefended and drinking lattes every day. This is not that story, though I wish it were. Because I do love Belle and now she has hair the color of a dead witch. Now she's gone and not told anyone where.

We did sleep. Oh, how we slept. We curled up in Belle's twin bed like sisters scared of the dark. The last time I saw her we also slept like that.

One night, during the last few weeks of college, we didn't meet up. We had homework or something. We drank bourbon and Coke in our own bedrooms. It got late. I fell asleep but then woke hyper, buzzed, tingly. It was midnight. I didn't text anyone. No reason. If I had given it any thought, I would have known then it was all ending, that our self-imposed solidarity was wearing thin.

Do not be tempted to think of me in this moment as some butterfly breaking free. We were not and are not butterflies. Do not picture orange wings. There were no orange wings.

You may imagine me as leaking caterpillar soup. You know, the point in a butterfly's life cycle when a caterpillar has eaten itself alive, dissolved itself with its own digestive juices and is stew, an eyeball floating next to an antenna. A secret I did not tell my kindergartners when I still taught: some caterpillars stay soup.

I do have some rocks from that night in the box.

It was an hour until closing at the Treehouse and it was packed. I ordered a drink and went to the dance floor. Maybe fifteen minutes later, Rickey and I spied each other and waved, but I didn't stop dancing in the patch of empty space I'd claimed near the girls' restroom. I used a straw to sip my white Russian. The sweetness burned my throat. Rickey was talking to this bro from poli sci, the one she had called an asshole after his presentation on John Locke. I wondered where Ricki-*baby* was.

I ignored the smell of vomit and rum punch. I danced. My land-locked body moved as loose as a forty-peso gypsy scarf blowing in the breeze next to a stall of hanging meat shanks. That night, my body was on vacation. Albeit a kind of crappy one, a staycation.

The lights came on. The jarring silence drove everybody into the night. That's when I saw her again. Rickey was kissing that bro.

All around me, tipsy students piled into their cars, kicking up gravel as they revved out of the Treehouse's lot. Dust swirled under the yellow sodium lights, and Rickey was still kissing that bro.

I stormed up to them, grabbed her hand, and pulled. But her mouth was stuck to his.

"Rici, leave me alone. I'm fine," she hissed.

She pushed me. Not that hard, but enough. I walked away, but they started back up again. Kissing. And I reached down and flung handful after handful of gravel at them until a truck caught me in its beams.

"Bitch!" some kids screamed out their window. And then I flung more pebbles at them and the truck's tailgate as it pulled away.

Just like that, Rickey and the bro were gone. The parking lot was empty. At least that's what I remember. That and I got a C on my organic chemistry final the next morning. Bye-bye, college.

We graduated.

WE STOOD IN front of a sea of white chairs, the Rickies plus an older sister in taffeta dresses, gerbera daisies and baby's breath in hand. We peered at Claire/Rickey standing two lengths ahead, swathed in silk the color of crème brûlée.

The pastor said, "You may kiss the bride," and as her now-husband, Jim, dipped and smooched her I wondered if he knew her name, her real name, the one she paid a hundred dollars for. It had only been three years.

The couple exited and we, the remaining Rickies, squeezed hands, until one by one we peeled off to walk down the aisle.

At the reception, the DJ announced the bridal party. His miked voice was too big for the room. My accompanying groomsman, some cousin, bolted to the bar. I didn't know where Ricki or Ricky were so I made a dash for the table of cupcakes and then realized maybe there was some tradition we were supposed to wait for, even though it was cupcakes and not a wedding cake. I had no clue. It was my first wedding.

The bro from that night at the Treehouse, who Claire dated for six months and now calls her BFE ("best friend ex") and who must drive Jim nuts because he still twirls and lifts Claire whenever he greets her, approached. I acted fast, grabbing a lemon meringue cupcake and sticking half of it in my mouth. Somehow I still ended up on the dance floor with him. Alongside Claire and Jim, Ricky and Ricki, a cartwheeling ring bearer, and twirling flower girls, we grinned and shouted the lyrics. I hadn't been with anyone since study abroad, and surrounded by friends I felt as brave as the choo choo in the story I read every first day of school to my students. I was the Little Rici Who Could.

I invited the maybe-bro outside into the cool night air. I wanted to cover his neck with my new burnt sienna lipstick (worn flat now but still in my makeup bag) or at least I wanted to want to, and so I did. His hands ran over the horrible bridesmaid dress, and instead of lumpy and tacky and scared I felt amazing. Well, okay.

When a few minutes later I had my hand on his zipper I realized I was moving with that same odd mix of painstaking carefulness and adrenaline as when I go to the gun range.

I unzipped his slacks and worked my way under his boxers and he managed to push down the top half of my green poofy dress. I felt like a half-naked Tinker Bell. And I was overtaken with belly-shaking laughter. So shocked and thrilled I was at our pale silly fleshiness that I couldn't stop laughing. His cock cradled in my hand was as light and sweet as a just-born kitten. It could be stamped out with my hand or underfoot, drowned in a milk bucket with no effort at all. Nothing ultra-scale or gunmetal gray about it.

I can't believe I just said that. Anyway, the maybe-not-so-much-a-bro smiled with me, though he probably didn't know at what, and we kept going.

We, no me, me and him, lay next to each other in the dewy grass. Naked-white and mouth-pink half-buds on gangly spring trees shone in the darkness, and I stared at them a bit longer before I went back to the party. Alone.

———

A FEW WEEKS later Belle and I started getting together again. She was nearby at her graduate program. Back then she had Rainbow Brite hair, a cheery ombré that went down her back. It was fun to see her. I often went out with my teacher friends for happy hour, but it's true what they say about women who teach elementary school: they are kind people who once dreamed of being dolphin trainers but are thrilled all the same to watch small children jump through hoops. Sometimes it was difficult to drink wine and pretend I did not want more. I had needed Belle more than I knew. When she talked about her classes I would think maybe I could go back to school too. We talked about ideas and books and sometimes even guys. It was so good to spend time with someone who had more than a three-minute attention span. One afternoon I noticed we'd both just said *and then*. I had been waiting so long for this that I'd forgotten I'd been waiting.

And then we will. And then. And then. And then.

That late afternoon, drinking $4 red wine at a coffee shop, was our moment in the sun. It had taken us longer than Ricki and Rickey, but we were okay. We had made ourselves anew and then anew again. We were Belle and Lisa. Maybe for a minute I even believed we were butterflies. And then we lived happily ever after.

OF COURSE, THAT's not what happened.

The Rickies thing was dead. Embarrassing, even. No one ever mentioned it. Not cheerfully centered Beth and certainly not married Claire. Now Belle and I didn't need it either. I put the stuff in the box and shoved it under my bed. I decided that, someday, if I had a daughter, I would explain that riding in cars (or rickshaws or scooters or buses) with boys isn't something she can avoid, but that with me she can be as ugly as she wants. She's never got to smile unless she feels like it. She can leave all her dark thoughts out in the open. I will take care of them.

I told Belle all this a couple years later when I was finishing up my second year at vet school and she took the train (she avoided buses) from Boston to Philadelphia to visit for the weekend. She had short-cropped hair dyed gray-purple and was writing her dissertation. She was on and off meds for depression and anxiety. She told me that in ancient Egypt women dyed their hair dark with walnuts mixed with the blood of a black cat and that "everything comes back."

"Belle, did something happen?"

"Everything comes back," she repeated.

I stole two of her Xanax. The world swam by for an hour. She told me she met a guy in the history department who was really cool until he wasn't, not at all.

"Report him," I said. "Do it."

She shook her head no. "Then that's all history will have to say about me."

We drank wine. I offered to sneak into this guy's condo and chop off his toe, because that's what has to be said when your friend tells you *it* happened again. She thanked me, and for a minute we wondered if we could do it. The breaking and entering. The threatening. The sawing through bone. But this isn't a movie, and Belle and I figured we didn't look good enough to get away with it if we got caught and ended up on the news.

We ate at a fancy Greek place where they served us a plate of cheese that was on fire, and she stuck her hand into the flame.

The waiter screamed. I dumped a glass of ice water on her.

"Sorry! Sorry!" she said. "I thought it was fake or something."

But I'm pretty sure that wasn't what she thought, that she wanted to burn herself alive for a second, as though she were nothing more than an effigy, a dummy of herself made for one purpose: to get rid of.

That's when I decided to show her the box under my bed. We added the receipt from the restaurant and a small piece of her blistered skin. She asked if she could send me her long rainbow ponytail, which was in her sock drawer.

"It doesn't feel right there," she said.

"What else have you been hanging on to?" I asked.

I haven't seen Belle since that night. We finished another bottle of wine. I took my Ambien. We went to sleep in my queen-size bed, holding on to each other, until one of us shifted, and then the other. Our backs to each other but our feet touching. When I woke up she was gone. Her phone on my bedside. Her backpack missing.

Her parents filed a police report. No one expected it to do any good.

It's been months, and here's the thing. I've started to wonder: if I left the box open next to my bed, if I ran my hands through it (the sweaters, the gravel, the letters, the dead skin and kitten claws), if I didn't put the lid back on it and instead let everything out—what would happen?

Could she find her way back to me?

Is she down there, inside the box somehow, drinking whiskey with the Rickies? Are they keeping her there?

I had told her the box keeps the Rickies alive, no matter what. And the Rickies keep us—Lisa, Belle, Beth, and Claire—alive. The Rickies live under my bed. They tame the ugly things. They are the ugly things. They are the bravest and worst pieces of us. They live in the dark on nothing but dust, so we don't have to. I hope she believed me. She said so herself: everything comes back. But I'm still waiting.

———————

Sarah Curry earned an MFA in fiction from Virginia Commonwealth University. Her work has appeared in *Nimrod International Journal*. Her fiction has been a finalist for the Center for Women Writers International Literary Award in Prose and the Francine Ringold Awards for New Writers. She is at work on a novel. She lives and works in Kentucky with her children and husband, a mathematician.

EDITOR'S NOTE

We are always searching for formally innovative work by new writers, and Kelsey Peterson's imaginary dialogue between the famous Pascal siblings serves as a distinctive example of such experimentation. A meditation on the origins of knowledge and spirituality, rendered in epistolary fragments brilliant as gemstones, the piece explores questions such as "Can God be found out?" and "What have we to fear when he tells us to fear nothing?" Beyond these existential themes, the siblings' mutual curiosity reveals much about the historical personages themselves and the minute intimacies of their relationship. With minimal, deft, seemingly effortless strokes, Peterson's piece is a remarkable achievement—not only a unique approach to narrative but as ambitious in conceit as it is successful in execution.

Bradford Morrow, Editor
Conjunctions

THE UNSENT LETTERS OF BLAISE AND JACQUELINE PASCAL

Kelsey Peterson

Blaise Pascal was a French mathematician and Christian apologist born in 1623. He was very close with his younger sister, Jacqueline, born in 1625, a poet who became a nun. Both were considered prodigies.

Brother,

I saw a perfect circle today. The yellow disk at the center of an anemone bloomed early and whose white petals had curled back in the wind. I marveled at its humble perfection, springing forth from some superabundance of the unrelenting spring. I am curious if there is an equation for such a flower, the formula to project its arcs and angles, its radii and planes. But I think: what an excessive, joyful thing. Let us smell it and give glory to God.

> Jacqueline,
> Printed in the *Gazette* today there was a poem of some merit, and I wondered if you still write. To

harness the imagination to your whimsy—it's
a dangerous, even dangerously useless gift, but
you ~~had~~ have it.

Port-Royal has seen a premature yield of flowers
and herbs, some eager but underdeveloped fruit.
I have been apprenticing in our little school, but
Mère Angelique wants me acquainted with all of
our abbey's operations, especially before I take
my vows.

> I don't doubt that Mère Agnes has dissuaded you
> from practicing it. Instead, you must be mending
> socks. The clink clink of your needles.

M. D'Andilly is a master gardener. He's cul-
tivated rows of espaliered pear trees, their
branches tamed to grow flat and straight as bou-
levards. As he trains the young trees, tying their
soft bendable limbs against the trellis, he pulls
and lashes them quite firmly.

> I'm writing because it's been six months since
> you left, and I thought—

I am far gentler, afraid they will break, but he
knows the stuff of which they're made. It's this
intimacy, more than any of his knowledge, that
tells me he's a master gardener.

Dear Jacqueline,

I wait for your letters, in the pattern they once arrived. I wonder how often you must pray to God.

From my room, I can sometimes smell the garden, if the wind is strong enough.

As you rise, your voice still hoarse, your face puffy.

In those moments, my happiness is greater than my own two arms spread wide.

Noon, your mind cast ahead to the thoughts of the day, back to what was left undone. At dusk, languor setting in.

Then I think: brother.

I am curious.

Are you still trying to measure the air?

Do you ask Him questions?

Are you still perfecting your triangle of chance?

Does He answer you?

Do you believe God can be found out?

I don't doubt that you believe He does.

Blaise, my brother,
I began to write you a letter, but I lost it. You
might wonder how, with so few possessions to
my name, I could lose something. The truth is I
carried it with me into the swamp.

Were we to speak as we once did, I would tell
you about magic numbers.

8	1	6
3	5	7
4	9	2

Sometimes I can feel what you describe as the
atmosphere in the swamp. I can feel how it is
different from in town. It's as though the air
is holding in water, bloated, sleepily weighed
down, slumping against the earth.

In this array of numbers, every integer in every direction adds up to the same number. This
number is called the magic constant. The magic
constant here, if you haven't figured it out yet,
is fifteen.

Somehow, I lost your letter in the swamp.

This arithmetic originates with the Chinese, who believed magic squares mirror some essential balance in the universe. They are inherently satisfying to produce, as if you've discovered some mystery that is, while invisible in the world, the very stuff that undergirds it.

I began to write again, a little ditty. I know you despise Poetry, but you don't despise my poetry. When I see the words on the page and hear in my mind the well-ordered, lilting lines of verse, I feel a small dose of the pleasure I'm sure God felt when he fashioned us out of dust and saw that we were good.

But I could not speak with you about this now.

I remember when I appeared before the queen and the princess. I was so young then. You were banging against our pots and pans and scribbling your thoughts on acoustics. Meanwhile, I had my own thoughts on acoustics: the flow and cadence of words confined to lines, bursting from lines, refracting each other's sounds as water does light.

You would condemn me.

I remember improvising verse for her highness, an exercise like embroidering in my head, a more satisfying reward in itself than the treats

they gave us to follow, the tart lemonade and the
shining cherries.

> Dear Sister,
> You won't believe it, but I sold another one of
> my machines—the "Pascaline"! I know you
> found it, I believe your words were, "as cum-
> bersome as a cow in labor," but I believe the
> gentleman, a tax collector in Paris, will find it
> perfectly functional.

Brother,
I am so hateful. I am—I hate myself. I write a
poem and I am smitten, as though I were the one
who held the waters in a span and with a look
tamed the Leviathan. And then! I return again
to the pen. Like a dog to its vomit.

> There are times when, as I draw close to num-
> bers, as I learn to fine-tune and predict them,
> I find there is no knowing them. Numbers are
> immortal. They sprawl.

Living water will never issue from my pen. All I
set down will be dried up. And while I am agog
in my poesy, I am oblivious to the one who makes
the sun to shine and gives the flowers growth.

> I come close, as one comes close to a person,
> only to realize, on the physical level, I will never

consider each hair and freckle on their body, and
within those tissues and follicles, blood rushes
and humors balance, and within those, atoms
break into tinier iotas;

But most hateful—I must let go this hate—is
that I left.

and then, on the spiritual level, there are
thoughts and subthoughts I will never know;
even the memories and ways of thinking that
create those thoughts; even the structures of the
mind and the hidden waxings of the soul that
produce those impressions . . .

I left without saying goodbye. In the morning, as
though for a walk, before you had woken.

And so, accepting that I will never know a person—let alone distance, abandonment, death—
I turn to the world of numbers, thinking I can
surely know them; they are still, steadfast,
immutable;

I made my promise to Father that I would stay
until he passed. And so I did. And then, beyond
that, I remained with you, for your good. But I
am not the means to your well-being, although
you may—I know you can—think so.

but they prove just as eternally, minutely recur-
sive, and forever, frustratingly teeming.

What is my love unto God if my hands and feet,
my body and soul, are unto you—

I think: what am I to do.

soaking cloths in brandy for your constant, constant ailments, spooning food into your mouth,

I think: I have made this machine. I have tin-
kered and prodded, set levers just so, produced
an object that without me will produce.

and once you're well, sweeping the hall while you
disappear to salons, returning to regale me with
visions of turkey rugs, stacked porcelain chips,
silver tureens lifted to reveal steaming pheasants.

Surely, others will create machines more complex, capable of dividing and then some, perhaps
even grasping the whole world of numbers.

There are two loves, Blaise.

But will a machine be in awe of that world?

One for God, one for self.

Will a machine delight in such emergent, barely perceptible knowledge, the way the sun appears as a mirage of golden gel on the water before it rises?

Mère Agnes told me I must hate my genius.

They will never know what it is to know something new. To be made new by knowing something.

I showed her my latest ditty. And I think,

Our God is hidden. He rewards those who seek him.

I do hate my genius—my needy, clamoring genius.
But I love ~~him~~ it too.

Sister,

Brother,

I don't understand the opposition to the existence of a vacuum. My experiments, especially with Florin's help on the Puy de Dôme, provide incontrovertible evidence that they exist. One would think people would sooner deny their ability to see—see the silver mercury dip in the long glass tubes as they were carried, precariously, tilting, up the mountainside—than they would revise their prior way of thinking.

Christ showed himself to children. I learn more about him through crude acts of daily routine than I do reading the volumes M. Arnauld copies from Latin. Our Lord was a carpenter, not a scholar. His hands knew the grain, knew splinters; they were not soft.

Come. Let us say God could not create a vacuum. Let us say God could not even sustain a vacuum, for how can he be everywhere when not everywhere allows him to be?

I lift myself from sleep. I fill my bowl with pottage.

Now. In the beginning, we are told, God created the heavens and the earth ex nihilo.

I adjust my veil. I wipe sweat from my chin.

What were his materials? Nothing. What was his model? Nothing. What have we to fear when he tells us to fear nothing?

I quench my thirst with beer.

I fear not lack of certainty—for who in this life
has certainty?

I sprinkle my parchment with pounce.

I fear God has forsaken me,

I grind thistle leaves to powder.

as you have.

I suck my thumb from jamming it in the door.

I fear all I have accomplished is a vapor.

I throw my shovel in the wet earth. I hold a girl's
foot by the heel; I wipe away the pus from an
open sore.

I wish you would not think of me as a vapor. As
something that should not be held.

I dry my socks on the back of a chair. I wake in
the night from a dream, and I cannot feel my arm.

If you can, think of me not as your brother.
Think of me not as the diseased, as the gam-
bling, as the genius.

I find in my hair a dead spider.

> Think of me as a student you teach. Think of me
> as knowing nothing, yet knowing everything.
> Think of me as innocent, yet guilty. Think of me
> as before my time, yet hurtling toward it.

I give, to a girl, a pair of socks. I lick from my
lips the sweet wine from the cup.

> Think of me growing old, then growing young.
> Think of me gaining strength, then losing it. Think
> of me groping toward knowledge, yet knowledge
> evading me. Think of me hating, yet loving.
> Think of me hating myself, yet loving myself.
> Think of me hating the world, yet loving the
> world.

I see my reflection in the still water of the bog. I
squeeze my eyes against a headache.

> Think of me dying, yet living.

Lord, run to me.

> There are two loves, Jacqueline.

That is my prayer.

> One for God, one for neighbor.

Lord, run.

Think of me as your neighbor.

I will take my vows.

Dear Jacqueline,

"The fear of the Lord is the beginning of wisdom."

I will stake my life on it.

––––––––––

Kelsey Peterson is assistant teaching professor of English at Pennsylvania State University. Her work has appeared or is forthcoming in *Conjunctions*, *West Branch*, and *Meridian*, and she was a finalist for the 2019 Chautauqua Janus Prize. She holds an MFA from Washington University in St. Louis, where she was an Olin Fellow. She lives in Boalsburg, Pennsylvania, with her husband.

EDITOR'S NOTE

Panel 1: In the corner of this panel, a rectangular box reads "Spring 2018, The English-Philosophy Building at the University of Iowa." Inside the cozy office of *The Iowa Review*, the fiction editor sits stunned at her computer, mouth agape. She is reading blind submissions for the annual *Iowa Review* Awards and has found a true gem among the slush pile. Though she is tall, amazement renders the fiction editor's head bigger than her body. Her glasses are half-obscured by white sparkles. The background of this panel is pastel, which is a shame, since this comic will be printed in black and white.

Panel 2: In front of an all-black background, a large thought balloon cluttered with text: "I can't believe it . . . a story called 'The Manga Artist' that isn't a) a fetishistic exploration of Japanese culture, b) a mockery of a wide-ranging, diverse medium, or c) a cute experiment? This is an amazing piece of work, effectively conveying the many delights of manga without a single drawing. Instead, 'The Manga Artist' verbalizes the pictorial language and formal constraints of manga to compress time but maximize emotion, painting a complete picture of longing, loneliness, queer love, and heartbreak across the traditional canvas of the short story. We need to publish this! Who are you, mystery author!? Can we trade manga recs!?"

Panel 3: A crosshatch-heavy collage containing images of Alexander Chee's congratulatory blurb and a close-up of the name "Doug Henderson" featured as a contest runner-up within the pages of *The Iowa Review* Winter 2018/19 issue. Inside a white rectangle placed at the bottom of the page, a message: "Sometimes, a good story leaves us speechless. 'The Manga Artist' is one of those stories."

Alexa Frank, Fiction Editor
The Iowa Review

THE MANGA ARTIST

Doug Henderson

Panel 1: The English teacher stands in front of his class. He is smiling and relaxed, leaning against his desk. Over his shoulder, the
whiteboard reads: You can go to London. You can go to Paris. But
you can't go to shopping.

He is blond with blue eyes, young and fresh-faced, a more idealized version of myself. He doesn't have to pluck the space between
his eyebrows or lose those last five pounds.

His top button is undone. His tie is loose. His shirtsleeves are
rolled up, exposing his hairy forearms. Chest hair rises above his
collar, sandy and golden. He is exotic to his students. They never
knew blonds could be hairy. He is teaching more than language.

Panels 2–5: The teacher is speaking, but there are no word balloons.
What he is saying isn't important. He is teaching in the way that
American college students spending a summer abroad do, with an
emphasis on charm, on telling jokes, and on winning the class over.
The smiles on the student's faces make it clear they are entranced.
To watch him move, to be in his presence, is reason enough for the
class to meet three times a week.

Panel 6: Of the ten students drawn, eight are women; two are men.
The men are in dark suits with jackets and ties. Their ties are not

loose. The women are a mix of old and young. Some are dressed for the office; some are in trendy street clothes.

In the earlier panels, the students were smiling, enchanted; now they are shocked. Some look annoyed. They dart their eyes to the right, toward the back of the classroom.

Above their heads floats the first word balloon. Its tail points off the panel to a speaker yet unseen.

"That's not what I learned."

Panel 7: Masashige is sitting in the back of the class beside the windows. He is grinning and leaning back in his chair. He is stocky with a broad face. His hair is buzzed in an attempt to hide his receding hairline. He has a sparse five o'clock shadow and a short goatee on his chin. No mustache. He is not wearing a suit. He is wearing the baggy striped T-shirt he always wore. As he smiles, his cheeks dimple and his eyes crinkle.

"In my company, we use 'due date,' not 'deadline,'" Masashige says.

Panels 8–9: The English teacher is smiling as he sits casually on his desk. He is unfazed by Masashige's challenge because Masashige always challenges him.

With a wave of his hand, the teacher says, "Both are okay."

The matter is settled then. The students are relieved and smiling again.

Panel 10: Masashige and the teacher look at each other across the room while the other students chatter and collect their books. The teacher is still smiling. Masashige is still grinning within the sunbeam. Something undrawn is passing between them.

THE MANGA ARTIST 49

Panels 11–12: The bell rings. Faceless students file into the hall. On the wall is a bulletin board with photos and profiles of all the teachers.

Panel 13: The English teacher's profile and photo are second from the left. His shirt collar is buttoned. His tie is tight. His name is Scotty James. He is an American from Cleveland, Ohio. His favorite color: sky blue. His favorite movie: *The Empire Strikes Back.* His favorite food: pepperoni pizza. His blood type: AB. His motto: Adventure every day! *Gambatte kudasai!*

Scotty never intended to teach English in Japan. He intended to become a graphic artist, but after graduating, jobs were scarce. When he saw a flyer offering a position teaching for the summer in Japan, he thought it was better than working retail. Teaching in Japan sounded exotic. And impressive. The kind of opportunity that could lead to anything.

Panel 14: Masashige's messy apartment sprawls across the panel, lush with detritus. Wooden beams line the ceiling, tatami mats pad the floor, and sliding paper doors stand slightly open. Empty bowls of instant ramen are stacked up like a miniature city on the *kotatsu.* Pushed against one wall is an angled drawing table with half-finished panels of a comic book. Beneath the desk sits an overflowing trash can. There are clothes on the floor and on the desk chair. Shelves crammed with books and manga and toys line the walls, but I couldn't possibly draw all the figurines Masashige loved to collect from vending machines and Happy Meals.

Pressed against the far wall, beneath the open window, is a futon occupied by two naked bodies.

Panel 15: Scotty and Masashige lie on their backs looking content and restful. Masashige is running a hand through the hair on Scotty's chest. Their bodies are not drawn in great detail, but it is clear that Masashige is circumcised while Scotty is not. A twist that surprised us both.

Panels 16–17: Lazy word balloons hang from the top of the panels.

"You don't care if they suspect us?" Scotty asks.

"They won't." Masashige's eyes are closed. "They are typical Japanese."

Because Masashige graduated with a degree in fine art, he thought of himself as separate from other Japanese, even though he had yet to do anything with his art and worked part-time serving drinks at a café.

"By the way, I started drawing a new manga," Masashige says. "It's about a mouse named Alfonso."

Panels 18–19: An empty classroom in an elementary school. The small chairs are tucked neatly against the desks. The chalkboard has been cleaned. On the teacher's desk there is a vase with flowers. Late-afternoon sun filters through the windows.

A word balloon floating in the right-hand corner says: "Alfonso lives in the wall of a third-grade classroom."

A mouse scurries across the floor beneath the desks and chairs, past the low shelves stocked with books. He is gray with white paws and black eyes. He stands on his hind feet and slides a book from the shelf. Its spine is thin and more than twice his height.

"He taught himself to read by listening from the back of the class."

Panel 20: Alfonso is on top of the open picture book. The words are in Japanese, but the story is simple. A pig is rolling in mud on one page. A duck is swimming in a pond on the other.

In word balloons pointing off the page, Masashige narrates, "Reading is not popular among the mice, but Alfonso thinks in the future all mice will need to read."

Panels 21–22: "Every evening, Alfonso sneaks into the class and reads a book, until one day . . ."

Alfonso is running along the windowsill, past potted plants and stacks of books, when he stops abruptly.

In front of him is a large glass aquarium. The bottom is filled with wood chips. Pressing against the glass, standing on its hind legs, is a hamster. It is white with gray ears.

"*Konnichiwa,*" reads a word balloon written in Japanese.

Underneath, a second balloon pointing off the page is written in English.

"His name is Ham Sandwich."

Panel 23: Scotty and Masashige are standing over the drawing table, still naked. Scotty is holding the panels of Masashige's manga and looking at them with a smile, but he is not only impressed, he is jealous. Scotty hasn't drawn anything since he arrived in Japan.

"Why Ham Sandwich?"

Masashige says, "The teacher bought him as a present for the class, and the students chose the name. They thought it was funny. They call him Hamuchan."

Panels 24–25: "From now on, Alfonso reads a book to Hamuchan every night and they become friends. Hamuchan only knows about the pet store and his glass box."

"Does Hamuchan ever get out?" Scotty asks. He skips ahead to the end of the story, but it isn't drawn yet.

Masashige says, "Maybe, but I don't know how."

Of course he didn't. Masashige never finishes any of the manga he draws. Straight out of college, he got a temporary job as an assistant at a manga house, but he never drew anything more than backgrounds and scenery. He talked about publishing his own manga independently. He said several times, "I'm going to rent a booth with my friend at the next Fujieda manga fair."

But I don't know if he ever did.

Panels 26–30: Scotty is walking in a clean, modern downtown, past restaurants and shops. The signs on the buildings are all in Japanese except one: Fujieda Station.

As he walks, Scotty talks into his cell phone.

"Yes, Mom, everything is great. Yes, it's safe. No, everyone does not speak English." He stops and looks in the window of a restaurant to check out the plastic models of the food they serve. "Yes, they have grocery stores. Yes, they ride bicycles. It's like any other first-world country. Don't worry. Everything is fine. I'm like a local already. I'll send some pics."

He chooses a restaurant and bows beneath the curtains that hang in the doorway. The restaurant is packed with low chairs and tables. Customers are hunched over steaming bowls of noodles. At the far end is an open kitchen where a lone chef is cooking behind a counter.

Scotty takes a seat. There are no menus. No waiter or waitress arrives to take his order. He looks confused. From above his left shoulder floats a word balloon. It is not filled with Japanese. It is filled with chicken scratch.

The cook, in a dirty apron, is talking to Scotty from behind the counter. He is scowling and motioning with a spatula.

"Tempura soba?" Scotty asks.

The cook, shouting in chicken scratch, points toward the door.

Panel 31: A vending machine near the entrance is embedded into the wall. Scotty stands before it. The front is filled with large rectangular buttons. All of the writing is in Japanese and there are no pictures. There is a slot for coins and bills, and at the bottom is an open area where something will drop out. A line has begun to form behind Scotty as people, bowing beneath the curtain, try to enter the restaurant.

The cook is shouting. Customers are looking up from their meals and watching Scotty fumble with the machine. There are beads of sweat on his brow.

Panel 32: Scotty is at McDonald's eating a hamburger. To his right is a bag of fries and to his left a large drink. He looks satisfied.

Panel 33: An open door at the end of a long, dark hallway. On the door is a nameplate: TEACHER LOUNGE.

Panel 34: The teacher's lounge has a sofa and several tables with chairs. There are no windows. The walls are covered with bookshelves. Scotty sits at one of the tables, surfing on his phone and eating a sandwich. There are several other teachers with him, two men in shirts and ties and a woman in a blouse and skirt. They are all Westerners. They sit at a small table next to Scotty and eat with chopsticks out of plastic bento boxes.

The two male teachers are talking.

"What do you think of Misako?" Thomas, the bigger one, asks.

"Who?" Scotty's mouth is full, but the word balloon is pointing at him.

"She works for the travel bureau. Wants to move to Australia."

Panel 35: An image of a woman with long dark hair and a slim face floats above Scotty's right shoulder.

Panel 36: Scotty is working at his desk. Misako is standing on the other side, looking at him attentively. Behind her, other students file out of the classroom. Her hands are outstretched, presenting Scotty with a cellophane bag of mini chocolate chip cookies.

"Scotty sensei, this is for you."

Panel 37: Sitting in the teacher's lounge, talking with the guys, Scotty says, "She's all right, but I wouldn't do her."

The teachers throw back their heads, and "HAHAHA" arches above the panel.

They know Scotty is gay. He came out to them during their first week of orientation. It was never his intention to go back into the closet when he arrived in Japan. But he hasn't come out to the students. Masashige, who pinged his gaydar, being the only exception.

The school feared teachers would steal clients by tutoring them privately, so having lunch or even a cup of coffee with a student was not allowed. Certainly having sex with them was out of the question. But in Fujieda, there are not many places for foreigners to mix

with the Japanese, or for the Japanese to mix with foreigners. And
the students were eager for contact. So, teachers taught in their free
time. They met up with students in the bars on the weekends. They
fucked the women crazy and broke their hearts.

Scotty decided during his first week in orientation not to be that
kind of teacher. If he met a guy, he would keep it simple.

Panel 38: Stars sparkle in the sky above a narrow street with low
wood-slat buildings. Neon signs written in English and Japanese
advertise BEER and SAKE. There are no cars, only the silhouettes of
people. There are no faces in the darkness.

Panel 39: One building is cleaner than the rest. Its facade is a lighter
wood. It has no windows, but its door is open. A sign, like a light
box, stands to the right. It reads: FRUITSBASKET. There are no rainbow flags or pink triangles, but this is Fujieda's most popular gay
club.

Panel 40: Masashige and Scotty are sitting together at the bar.
Scotty is dressed in his shirt and tie. Masashige is wearing stripes.
They are smiling, dimples out, stars in their eyes, and talking in
word balloons while they drink. Behind them, silhouettes dance.
Musical notes float above their heads.

Masashige says he has never been inside Fruitsbasket before.
Scotty asks why, but Masashige says he doesn't know.

"Don't you want to meet guys?" Scotty asks. "Don't you get
horny?"

Masashige says, "This place is not interesting."

But Scotty knows what Masashige means: Masashige isn't into
Japanese men.

Panels 41–44: Scotty takes Masashige by the hand and leads him onto the dance floor. It is crowded, but they find a space. Scotty raises his drink high, closes his eyes, and tries to lose himself in the music. Masashige is dancing too, but he does not stop watching Scotty.

Scotty takes off his tie and shoves it into his back pocket. He untucks his shirt and undoes another button. His sleeves are already rolled up. As he dances, the lights catch the hair on his forearms and the hair on his chest where his shirt is open.

Soon Scotty is surrounded by dancing men. Some have their shirts off. Some whisper in his ears. They put their arms around him. They try to reach their hands under his shirt.

Scotty looks for Masashige, but he is gone.

Panel 45: Scotty finds Masashige outside by the front door.

"Sorry," Masashige says, his word balloon low at the bottom of the panel. "I needed some air."

Panel 46: Masashige and Scotty are naked in bed. The panel shows them from the chest up.

"Is this getting too serious?" Scotty asks.

Panel 47: They lie in the dark, looking at the ceiling.

Panel 48: Masashige closes his eyes and says, "The gay world is sad."

Panel 49: Scotty pulls Masashige close, and they wrap their arms around each other.

Panel 50: They lie in the dark, pressed together.

Panels 51–55: Masashige and Scotty are walking through down-town Fujieda, near the station, past the shops and restaurants. The day is bright and sunny.

They enter the restaurant with the strange machine. Masashige casually stands before it and inserts coins in the slot. Scotty watches in wonder as Masashige presses a few buttons, and two tickets fall out. Masashige takes the tickets to the cook behind the counter, who nods in response, and then Masashige and Scotty take a table against the wall.

Panel 56: From a black portfolio, Masashige pulls out the pages of his manga.

"Alfonso reads to Hamuchan every day after school, but one day there is a girl staying late. Alfonso waits for her to leave, but instead she goes to Hamuchan's aquarium."

Panels 57–58: A giant hand reaches into the aquarium. Hamuchan is pressed against the glass, his eyes wide, but he cannot escape.

Hamuchan is lifted into the air by the giant hand. He watches from over the fingers as the ground falls away beneath him.

Panel 59: Alfonso runs into the classroom from his hole in the wall. The schoolgirl looms over him. She is dressed in a dark blue sailor uniform with a short skirt and long white socks pulled up to her knees. Hamuchan peeks out of her cupped hand.

Panel 60: The girl screams as Alfonso runs at her feet. She clutches her chest, dropping Hamuchan, who falls in a white blur against the blue uniform.

Panels 61–62: Hamuchan hits the floor and scurries to Alfonso. Together they run for the hole in the wall. Jagged word balloons float above them as the girl shouts in thick black letters: "*Nezumi! Nezumi!*"

Panel 63: The cook behind the counter yells something in chicken scratch. Masashige stands up and collects a tray with two steaming bowls of noodles and broth.

Scotty is reading the manga and flipping through the pages.

Panel 64: Alfonso and Hamuchan are walking inside the walls of the school, in the gap between the wood paneling, and Alfonso's world is revealed. Streams of mice are bustling back and forth along the beams above and below Alfonso and Hamuchan. Some carry pieces of food in their mouths. Some carry scraps of cloth or wood. They are big and small, brown, white, and gray. They rush past Alfonso and Hamuchan without a glance.

Hamuchan stands on his hind feet, taking in the scene. He is amazed.

Panel 65: Scotty looks at the pages of Masashige's manga with one hand while leaning over his bowl and shoveling noodles into his mouth.

"They have some adventures together," Masashige says from the other side of the table.

Panel 66: Over Scotty's shoulder, the mice in the manga are curled up in rice bowls, sleeping, only to be woken up and chased away by a screaming teacher.

In another panel, Alfonso shouts, *"Abunai!"* when Hamuchan chews on a wire.

"Demo oishii desu," Hamuchan says, looking embarrassed, the wire still hanging from his mouth.

A word balloon floats at the bottom of the page.

"Alfonso yells, 'That's dangerous!' And Hamuchan says, 'But it's delicious.'"

Panels 67–68: "This is adorable," Scotty says from over the pages. He thinks maybe he'll draw a manga someday, if he can come up with a good idea. "What are you going to do with it?"

"Remember I told you about the Art Institute in Chicago? I'm thinking to use this for my application."

Scotty does not remember, but he says, "You totally should."

"It's not done yet." Masashige takes the pages back. "But I have until December to apply."

Scotty will return to Cleveland at the end of August, in less than two months. By December, Japan and English teaching will be a memory, that crazy thing he did one summer.

"I hope I get to read the ending," Scotty says, his mouth full.

Panel 69: Scotty and Masashige slurp up their noodles. Steam rises from their bowls.

From behind the counter, the cook calls out another order in chicken scratch.

Panel 70: A bullet train speeds through the Japanese countryside. Green hills roll behind it. Mount Fuji rises in the distance against the blue sky.

Panel 71: Scotty and Masashige are sitting side by side on the train. Masashige is asleep, his head on Scotty's shoulder. Scotty is wearing sunglasses, his sketch pad on his knee as the rice paddies go by.

This is his first time outside of Fujieda since he arrived in Japan. He has only seen rice paddies in photos. He wanted them to be more interesting, but coming from Ohio, he is used to seeing the countryside, and he can't get excited over long swathes of nothingness. He has not sketched a thing. Who lives out here? he wonders. Who takes care of all this rice? He is thankful he didn't end up in a town more rural than Fujieda.

Panel 72: Scotty and Masashige are lost and confused, dragging their luggage through a hastily drawn sea of people. Every square foot of space is taken up by another person. There is no chance to stop; there is barely time to breathe.

In English above their heads are the words TOKYO STATION.

Panel 73: Scotty and Masashige are looking out of their cab as it sits in traffic. The neon lights of Tokyo reflect off the passenger windows: SONY, MASSAGE, LIVE SHOW, and TOSHIBA.

Panel 74: Scotty and Masashige are in a crowded clothing store. They are trying on silly hats and jackets and looking at the price tags with shocked expressions.

Panel 75: Scotty and Masashige are eating crepes rolled and stuffed with fruit and cream. Behind them, girls in black frilly dresses and top hats walk arm in arm beneath their lace parasols.

Panel 76: Scotty and Masashige are sitting on a sofa in a small square room and belting into a microphone. Music notes rise above their heads. The walls are decorated like an ocean beach, but through the window, sparkling skyscrapers reach toward the moon.

Panel 77: Scotty and Masashige are wandering down a dark, narrow side street. There are doorways on either side with men smoking in the shadows.

Panel 78: Scotty and Masashige have come to an intersection with a bar on every corner. One of the bars has a large open patio, and men have spilled into the street. The men are laughing and smiling. Some hold drinks. Some hold each other. Most are Japanese, but a good number are Westerners.

Scotty and Masashige exchange hungry smiles.

Panel 79: Scotty and Masashige are dancing. They have stripped off their shirts and are surrounded by musical notes and bare-chested men. Lights flash above them and music pounds out of the speakers in squiggly lines.

Panel 80: Scotty stands at the bar and watches while Masashige dances with a bearded, muscular man. Curly red hair covers the man, front and back. Masashige keeps his eyes lowered, trying to play it cool. But Scotty is smirking. He knows what Masashige likes.

Panel 81: Their arms around each other, Scotty and Masashige stumble out of the bar and flag down a taxi as the bearded man waves goodbye. Their cheeks are pink, their eyelids are heavy, asterisks spark around their heads, but they are smiling with satisfaction.

Panel 82: Scotty and Masashige are in their hotel room having sex. Masashige is lying back on the bed, and his legs are over Scotty's shoulders. Scotty's hairy butt fills the bottom left corner of the panel as he thrusts into Masashige. "AH AH AH" sprinkles the page.

Panels 83–84: Scotty collapses on top of Masashige. They are both huffing and puffing, but eventually their heartbeats slow down. Their bodies press together.

   "I love you," Masashige whispers.

   "I love you too," Scotty says.

   Their word balloons are small and perfectly round.

   These two panels are sketched in pencil. I never inked them. Heavy black lines cross through them.

Panel 85: Scotty and Masashige are back on the bullet train leaning against each other. This time they are both asleep.

Panel 86: Large black crows sit on a power line and "KAW KAW KAW." Below them, a trash bag they have torn open spews garbage into the street.

Panel 87: Scotty is sitting behind his desk wearing his shirt and tie. Afternoon sun pours through the windows. The classroom is empty of students except for Masashige, who stands on the other side of the desk.

"How have you been?" Masashige asks.

"I'm good," Scotty says.

"Why don't you answer your phone anymore?"

Panel 88: This is the conversation Scotty has been dreading since he arrived. He looks at Masashige with regret. A word balloon floats at the top of the page.

"I'm leaving in a few weeks."

Panel 89: "So, you don't want to see me?" Masashige asks in the center of one small panel.

Panel 90: "Of course I want to." Scotty looks out the window as he speaks.

Panel 91: "Just one more time," Masashige says.

Panel 92: Still Scotty looks out the window. His eyes are lowered. There is no word balloon.

Panel 93: "How about tomorrow night?" Masashige asks. "I'll cook dinner. Meet me in front of the *convini* at seven."

Panel 94: Scotty continues to look out the window, his eyes still lowered.

"Okay."

Panel 95: Two men are smoking in front of Fruitsbasket as Scotty walks into the darkness of the open doorway. It is night, and a few stars are visible in the sky. There are no cars passing, and no people walking by.

Panels 96–98: Scotty sits by himself at the bar and drinks. In each successive panel, his eyes become heavier, his posture more slouched.

"*Konnichiwaaa,*" he says when a man sits beside him.

Panel 99: Masashige is waiting outside a brightly lit convenience store. He holds a plastic bag filled with groceries. He is looking at his watch.

Panels 100–102: Scotty is on the dance floor. His shirt is open, and his tie is gone. Japanese men are dancing around him, touching him.

Scotty takes one of the men by the hand and leads him off the floor. He pulls the man into the restroom and into a stall.

The walls of the stall run from floor to ceiling. There are no gaps above or below. This allows for privacy.

Panel 103: Scotty's head is back and his eyes are closed. A hum of pleasure escapes his lips. The man's head bobs as it blocks Scotty's crotch from view.

Above Scotty's right shoulder floats an image of himself. He is looking at a small toy bear from Masashige's collection. Masashige watches from behind.

Panel 104: Scotty stands in Masashige's apartment, the toy bear in his hand as he studies it.

"Just so you know, this is only a summer fling."

Masashige, nodding, asks, "Fling *wa nani?*"

Panel 105: "It's just for fun," Scotty says, putting the bear back on the shelf among the other toys. "Just for right now. Let's not get serious."

Panel 106: "*Wakarimashita*," Masashige says, smiling. "I got it."

Panel 107: Masashige is sitting on the curb in front of the convenience store. The bag of groceries sits beside him. He is looking to his left, down the street, in the direction Scotty usually walks from.

Panel 108: Scotty steps into the panel. His clothes are disheveled. His head is down. His word balloon is small.

"Hey."

Panels 109–110: Scotty and Masashige are having sex on Masashige's futon. The room is dark. Their bodies are drawn in thick, curving lines. Their expressions are pained. Afterward, they lie back-to-back. Their eyes are open. Neither one can sleep.

Panel 111: Hanging from a flagpole, several colorful windsocks shaped like fish blow in the breeze.

Panel 112: It is a bright sunny day. Scotty and Masashige are hugging in front of Fujieda Station. On the curb behind them are two suitcases.

"Take care," Masashige says.

"Let me know about Chicago," Scotty says, but he doubts

Masashige will really apply for grad school. He doubts they will ever meet again.

Panel 113: On the airplane, Scotty sits beside a window. He is talking to a Japanese woman sitting to his left. He is smiling, all charm.

"I was an English teacher."

Panel 114: Clouds pass by outside, but Scotty isn't looking.

On his tray table is the manga Masashige drew.

Panel 115: Alfonso and Hamuchan have left the school. They are running down the wide front stairs, fear and excitement in their eyes. Before them a field of wild grass stretches tall and terrifying beyond the final edges of the page.

———————

Doug Henderson received his MFA from the University of San Francisco and lives in the Castro District with his husband and daughter.

EDITORS' NOTE

A very small percentage of the submissions we receive at *The Sun* end up being discussed by our editorial staff in a monthly meeting—that time is reserved for pieces that excite us and make us wonder how they might fit in the magazine. Laura Freudig's "Mother and Child" was one such submission. We recognized that a story where a mother leaves her infant alone in the elements might be a tough sell with our readers, but we were drawn to the sharp, witty voice—and the aching pessimism—of the narrator. There was a hard-won realism in the way Freudig told this story, and there were more than a few lines that just skewered us. One example among many: "For a long time that night, I watched the rise and fall of [my husband's] chest, thinking what a small raft are the words *I love you*." We marveled at the way Freudig captured the panic, the despair—the simple desire for *escape*—of motherhood, and were moved by the way she dealt with a very real dilemma faced by women. The story is grim, but it has a heart. The narrator isn't monstrous, nor is her husband, but she's overwhelmed by the expectations of who a mother should be.

As we'd hoped, our readers connected with the story. One, a new mother nursing her three-week-old, wrote in to say, "Freudig's story is one of the few that dares to tell the truth about just how difficult motherhood can be. . . . [It] conveys the more painful facets of the love between mother and child."

Carol Ann Fitzgerald, Managing Editor
Derek Askey, Assistant Editor
The Sun

MOTHER AND CHILD

Laura Freudig

MY HUSBAND, JOHN, calls me a good mother. He says this with a glint of unease in his eyes, as though he is telling a lie or working a charm. He calls during his coffee breaks—he doesn't drink coffee, so he has time to talk—and asks, "How is Clint?" and when I say, "Fine," or "Sleeping," or "Alive," he asks, "And how are you, sweetie?" He's learned that *sweetie* is a potent word. Still, my answers vary.

I know if he dared, he'd go next door to Humpback Ales after work and drink until I became bearable, which would be at least two hours for him, because he's a slow drinker. But he's home every day at 5:07 because he loves Clint, who is named after the ideal country lane where my husband grew up. He wants a similar childhood for his son, who may not be getting it.

Sometimes I answer my husband in what he calls a "truthful" way. I tell him what the baby and I did, how long his naps were, how much he ate. John likes me to be precise: three tablespoons of apricots, a bowl of rice cereal (that smelled of paste), one teething biscuit—nothing too small, nothing requiring teeth. John is very concerned about choking. Once, Clint did choke. I was feeding him, and suddenly he was gagging and turning blue, and his eyes were watering all down his messy cheeks. John was home and swooped him from his high chair and turned him upside down before I could blink. Then he yelled at me—as he was crying and clutching Clint—for not reacting quickly enough. Like I don't save that baby from death twenty times a day when he's not around. John says I'm careless with sharp objects; he probably thinks I'll let Clint run with scissors as soon as he becomes self-propelling. It's not really carelessness, though. More a curiosity about the properties of the knife's edge. When Clint was born, I cut the umbilical cord: it was strange to sever the thing that tethered us and to feel nothing.

But sometimes I answer my husband in a different way. I tell him what I'm really thinking, which doesn't have much to do with diapers and dusting and what to cook for dinner. I'm thinking: What if I fall down the basement stairs? What if John just left for work and won't be home for nine hours? There I lie, head smashed to a bloody yolk on the concrete floor, breasts mindlessly leaking milk as the baby screams. Or sometimes I'm thinking: What if I just leave? What if I take a bus ride with dirty strangers into gray twilight and get a hotel room whose door opens only onto endless hallways? I would wake every night to a phantom baby's cries, in a hot tangle of gritty sheets.

On days when I answer him that way, John walks around the house with the rabbity look in his eyes—twitchy, startled, dull—and pleads with me to tell him the truth. He doesn't understand that those are the days when I am.

TODAY WHEN JOHN calls, Clint is sitting in his blue bouncy chair on the kitchen floor. His eyes are dark, welling pools, and he shudders with the hiccups that follow a long cry. I'm glad John can't hear this, because he doesn't understand that sometimes babies just cry. They haven't necessarily been poked with a diaper pin or shaken or dropped.

"Hi, sweetie," he says. "How's your morning?"

I can hear voices in the background, the bell jangling on the front door, the photocopier's racket.

"Fine," I say from my perch on the kitchen stool. Out the window and across the field is a thin line of spruce trees, and through their branches the ocean glitters. We live on a small Maine island that tugs at its narrow bridge as if it longs to drift into the deeper Atlantic.

"What's Clint up to?"

"Just sitting."

"Where?" I hear a sharpness in his question, as if he thinks I've kept the baby in a cupboard all morning or balanced him on the brink of some household precipice.

"In his bouncy seat on the floor next to me."

"Oh, good. Got any plans today?"

"Let's see. Nursing, napping, changing. Maybe a little crying." That last one is a jab to get back at him for thinking I put the baby in a cupboard.

"You should go for a walk. Maybe go see Jana at the store." Jana is my sister-in-law.

"Do I have to take the baby?"

"Hannah!"

"Kidding. Maybe we will later. It's nap time." Is there any time that isn't nap time, or just before nap time, or just after nap time? Is there any space that is not occupied by Clint or my thoughts of him?

"Okay, sweetie. Call me if you need anything."

"We'll be fine. See you."

I say that every day: *We'll be fine.* But I don't believe it.

JOHN SELLS INSURANCE—AND buys a lot of it, too. He works down by the harbor for a paunchy man named Joe, who took over the business from his father, also named Joe, who took over from his father, named Joe. People whose insurance needs have spanned the careers of two Joes hardly blinked when one was carried out and the next took over. John sells safety to those who have too much to lose. His sales pitch skates the thin line between setting his clients at ease and reminding them of the forces of chaos that yearn to destroy their boats, houses, wives. I think this is how his clients see him: a steady young man who knows the price tag of their fears. ("She's priceless," they say of the boat, the house, the wife, but eventually they settle on a number.) If I worked there, I would tell them the worst things in the world are already inside the house, behind shut and locked doors.

It's like a drug, the adrenaline of disaster. I picture falling down the basement steps so clearly that it can't be a dream: My body is heavy and falls faster than thought, and the sixth stair, edged with splinters, comes toward my cheek like a board someone is swinging at me. I hear my baby cry from a long way off, but I am trapped in something wet and thick and can't reach him. The basement steps lead down into my future—dim, cobwebby, and uneven—where I lie, twisted, taking my last breath through shards of bone in my lungs. John will marry minty-mouthed Rosemary Nadeau (rhymes with *meadow*), who works in his office and sings soprano in the church choir. She'll wipe Clint's drool and clean the cheese paste from his crevices. Already she stands in a pool of sun at the top of the stairs, holding my baby on her hip. His tiny hand pats her hair.

"Just hold on to the railing," John tells me. And I do, usually.

BECAUSE WE GREW up in the same town, John thought he knew me. My mother and I moved to Maine when I was a girl. She was running north, as if what was chasing her could be left behind. Nobody brought casseroles to welcome us or stopped by with the name of the local pediatrician or the most reliable mechanic. In Maine you can live next door to someone for decades and never do anything but lift your fingers off the steering wheel in a casual wave when passing on the street. You can live on properties separated by a scraggly spruce tree and forty feet of weeds and know nothing of what goes on inside each other's houses. People here keep warm by holding their tongues.

Because I was pretty and well behaved, John thought I was good. But I was simply in the habit of doing what I was told: *Stand still. Shut up. Stop crying.* My mother said college for me would be a waste of money, since she'd already gotten me a job at the gas station—and where were her cigarettes? I wouldn't need a car, and she could use my employee discount. So I walked a half mile down broken asphalt to the gas station, to be embalmed in car exhaust and cigarette smoke. I rang up bruised apples, corn chips, and five gallons of unleaded without thinking I had a choice. Though what else I might have chosen remains unclear to me.

John didn't whistle at me or try to get me to laugh about how bad he'd been on the weekend or brush against me behind the rack of Slim Jims. Instead he bought orange juice and a pastry and asked me about the books I kept stashed under the newspapers by the cash register. His eyes were brown and calm.

"Hi, Hannah," he'd say in his kind voice. "Dostoyevsky, huh?" Or sometimes just "Beautiful day."

He thought I was cute and as sweet as a Danish in a cellophane pouch. I think he also found me mildly alarming, though the rabbity look was less pronounced then.

"You're not like anyone I know," he said, with just a ghost of reproach.

I WAS TEN years old and walking home from school. A squirrel zipped into the road, paused, then darted under the wheel of a passing car. The driver—the mother of one of my classmates—covered her mouth in mock apology, then waved to me and drove on. The squirrel's head was crushed, one eye popped whole from its socket, attached only by a twisted red thread. The eye *looked* at me, and I stared back until my mother stalked up the street, slapped me out of my trance, and shoved me home.

I told John that story on our twenty-fifth date, the one before the twenty-sixth, when he asked me to marry him. There was a long hiatus between those two dates, as if he was thinking about the implications for his future happiness.

On date number twenty-six we ate cake with plastic forks on a splintery bench by the pond. The gravel at our feet was green with algae and slick with goose droppings, and the geese cruised the water's dull surface, tracing out menacing patterns. John led me down a trail that wound around the pond. I didn't know quite what to expect, as our previous dates had all been indoors: the bowling alley, the pizza parlor, the movie theater, where he wouldn't stop kissing me. As we walked by the spot where the brown water sluiced over the dam, I thought, He is going to push me in. I heard my mother's voice singing a murderous ballad, her kind of lullaby: *He threw her in deep water, where he knew that she would drown.* All that kissing was leading somewhere.

But instead John went down on one knee in a mud puddle. I said yes quickly and pulled him to his feet. Our lips were dark with bittersweet chocolate, and the mud on his knee left a stain on my white sundress.

He wanted to have babies right away, so he bought a house for us, and I painted every room yellow. I don't know what I wanted— a little quiet, some fresh air, to get rid of my ugly and unpronounceable surname, a strong shoulder to lay my head on in the evenings, new dish towels that didn't belong to my mother. Every morning I drank my coffee with my left hand while John held my right.

As far back as I can recall, where memories are ragged and dreamlike, my mother pinched me black-and-blue in places that didn't show. Her voice droned furiously, like a television playing reruns at an unbearable volume. Now I swam in a stillness I'd never imagined could exist between two people in the same house.

I thought, I will never need to speak above a whisper.

John asked me if I wanted to go to college. Probably his older sister, Jana, had put him up to it. She—and the rest of his large, well-educated family—seemed friendly, but I knew what they said to each other: *He married that girl from the gas station. You've seen her mother, right?*

I didn't know what I should study, and John was no help. "Whatever you're interested in," he said, as though it was no struggle at all to imagine a different future.

"Maybe," I said, shrugging.

"Only if you want to, Hannah," he said with a smile.

I took a part-time job at the fabric store and put off applying to college until each semester's deadline had passed. The hours in that quiet place felt like a gift. I learned to sew. The bedroom next to ours, which was supposed to be a nursery, filled up with a cutting table, a sewing machine, and baskets of fabric. I sat there in the late afternoon with the warm, thick sun shining on me, my hands turning bright pieces of fabric into quilts, pillows, and wall hangings almost without a thought.

Every month the blood would come with a rush of something that felt a little like relief, a little like fear.

JOHN IS TALL enough to stand behind me and rest his chin on my head. He likes to do this. I do not know how I feel about it: cherished or pinned down.

Once, when he was standing that way, I asked him, "What if I never get pregnant?"

"What?" he asked, as though he hadn't heard me.

"What if I never get pregnant?"

"You will," he said.

"But what if I don't?"

He just walked away, and the top of my head was suddenly cold and untethered.

I WAS PREGNANT the next month, wretched and sick and wondering what could be growing inside me to make me feel so terrible. It couldn't be good. As the weeks passed, my belly swelled, but the rest of me seemed to shrivel around it, my tiny arms and legs waving. "I look like a tick," I said.

John smoothed my pale hair and told me I was more beautiful

than he'd thought possible—which, when you think about it, is a weaselly sort of compliment.

WHEN CLINT WAS born, I screamed in a voice that had never come out of my throat before, though it sounded familiar. It was my mother's scream, identical in pitch, timbre, and volume. Apparently the entirety of my childhood had been as painful to her as giving birth.

After Clint was born, I couldn't seem to stop screaming. Everything plagued me: my own tears, the smallness and squirminess of the baby, the number of objects in my house that were perfect for bashing in his tiny melon head.

YESTERDAY CLINT FUSSED from dawn to dusk. He whimpered. He made mewling coughs. He stiffened and sobbed.

When John got home, he lingered on the porch, as usual, arranged his shoes and briefcase in the entryway, hung up his coat and brushed off obscure hairs and particles of dust, studied the loose doorknob as if deciding how to fix it.

"Why do you just stand out there?" I yelled when he finally came inside.

He kissed me on the cheek and took the baby.

I long for my husband so desperately all day; then when he comes home, I am immediately furious with him.

"Go for a walk, Hannah," he said gently, "before it gets dark."

Go for a walk. That's his solution to every problem. I made a face at him, through my tears.

"Well, tell me, then," he said. "What do you want to do?"

He actually wants to know, I thought as he stood there, holding the baby in the crook of his arm, his eyebrows drawn together not in anger but concern.

"I don't know," I said.

But I went for a walk, even though what I think I really wanted was for John to put that baby in a bureau and quiet me with his hands and lick the salty tears from my lips. House lights winked on as dusk fell. I walked quickly, trying not to think. My mind, left to itself, is untrustworthy. That's what makes days with a wordless baby so perilous.

I walked to the end of our road and back. When I came in, John was feeding Clint applesauce. Slushy globs splattered the floor around the high chair. The baby was smiling and kicking his bare feet. John looked up, his expression hopeful, and said, "Feel better?" I began to cook dinner. Both of them stared sidelong at me all evening, like I was something that might disappear if you looked directly at it.

John always tells me he loves me just before he falls asleep: a nightly ritual. For a long time that night, I watched the rise and fall of his chest, thinking what a small raft are the words *I love you*.

THIS MORNING STARTS in the milky light just after dawn. John brings me the baby, who wiggles for a while, then settles into my arms. At the sharp tug of his mouth on my breast, the milk flows out, prickling. We doze until John leaves for work. Clint wakes dazed, sweaty, and fretful. I distract him with brightly colored toys, books, bananas, a bath, but nothing soothes him for long. I spend the next few hours trying to get him to sleep for more than twenty minutes, a span of time in which I can hardly muster the strength to do anything but breathe shallow, inaudible breaths. Whenever he wakes, I am hostage to his shattering voice, which seems like the same one I've heard all my life. There's no way to reason with that voice. I stand at the kitchen counter with a knife, wondering what I should cut: myself, my baby, or the loaf of bread on the board.

At one o'clock I buckle Clint into his jogging stroller and flee. Gravity pulls us down the hill at a run, stones sliding under my feet. The stroller veers sideways for a heart-clutching second. When the hill levels out, I push the panic down with slow breaths.

From here I can see the narrow channel winding through the mud flats as the tide creeps in. Above, the fall sky is the flat color of forgetting: a blue so thick it's impossible to picture the bitter months ahead, when each day is just a dim pall of gray light on snow.

The baby has calmed, too, and is making wet noises as he investigates his cheeks. Farther off I hear the whir of tires on the metal grating of the bridge, the drone of a lobster-boat engine, the high calls of gulls. Through the branches along the road, I glimpse a clearing like a green room, with sun-dappled walls of leaves and a moss-carpeted floor. I could step through the trees and lay Clint on the moss. He would touch its unfamiliar texture, and his laughter would bubble up as clear as a spring. But I continue down this hard road and don't turn aside.

A mile later we clatter across the bridge. Below the grating the water is green-black and ropy. Every time I drive over the bridge, I imagine the great, wallowing splash the car would make as it landed in the channel, how I would wrench Clint from his car seat and swim with him gripped under one arm toward the distant glimmer of the surface. The current would seize my legs, and my lungs would fill with frigid water. All buoyancy lost, we would sink into gray-green depths. Sometimes, though, I would escape through the broken windshield and crawl ashore alone.

Over the bridge is the general store, cobbled into a corner of the old sardine cannery. The door thumps shut behind me. John's sister Jana arranges a pile of receipts near the register. Her smooth brown hair is pulled into a knot; she looks a lot nicer from behind.

"Hi, Jana," I say.

She turns, a paper clip between her lips, the skin around her mouth crosshatched with lines. John says she never smoked; she's just addicted to a smoldering irritation. If he were here, she would steer him into an aisle to talk, but she only nods and waves a receipt at me.

There's just one other customer, a vaguely familiar woman who wanders the narrow aisles, looking up at me with a half-startled expression, as if trying to remember the fifth item from the list she left on her kitchen table. She's pretty in a pale, remote sort of way. She raises her hand to tuck a strand of hair behind her ear, and I realize I'm doing it, too. We turn away from each other at the same time.

The store smells faintly of bait, fryer grease, and fir sachets. Everything is twice the price and twice as old as in the supermarket down the road.

The pale, quiet woman disappears, but a minute later we spot each other again. She stops, as though she is going to speak. Then I realize I am staring into a mirror on the back wall. There is nobody else here. I didn't even recognize myself.

I buy an apple and a small bit of rope looped into a cloverleaf.

"They're coasters," Jana says. "People usually buy two or four."

I am planning to let Clint chew on it, but I don't tell her that.

"Maybe I'll have a bottle of water, too."

My *maybe* seems to annoy her. "Yes or no?" she asks, tapping a bottle on the counter.

I nod.

"Seven dollars."

Clint starts to twist and fuss in his seat, and I hand him the coaster as I fish in the pocket of the stroller for my wallet. Jana comes around the counter and crouches in front of him, tickling the underside of his chin until he laughs.

"I could keep him here with me for a while," she says without looking up. "It's pretty dead. Two people came in for lunch, and you and Clint make four. I'd like the company."

For a minute I think about saying yes. I think about the things I should cook, clean, and organize, and about the material in my sewing machine: blue canvas and silk. The needle is down, impaling them, and the seam has been an inch long for months. I'm not sure I remember how to work the levers, buttons, and dials. I think about the silence and how it would press against me. What if I don't want him back?

"I don't know," I say. "Maybe next time."

"Okay." She stands up. "You two have a good afternoon. Got any plans?"

"No, just a nap. It's been a rough morning." I feel my voice catch. I am naked in front of her. She knows how I watched the dust fall through the sunlight as the baby turned red with anguish.

"Bye, then," she says in a tired voice.

Near the door I say it, as quiet as dawn: "Help."

There's no reply. Did she hear me?

I push the stroller outside and maneuver Clint out of the straps and buckles to check his diaper. He kicks his legs and chews determinedly on the rope.

WALKING HOME IS almost more than I can bear. The stroller is like a block of stone on greased skids. It would be such a relief to let it slide away.

Clouds thicken in the west until the blue sky becomes a thin sliver on the horizon, then vanishes. Wind gusts across the road, blowing the blanket off the baby's lap. He falls asleep on the last hill and startles awake as the thunder begins.

The rest of the afternoon is the same: thunder, wind, rain, crying. The five-minute nap he took while I pushed him up the hill tricks him out of any more sleep. Eventually I cry, too, and Clint looks at me with saucer eyes and answers back with a flat, panicked wail.

I pick him up and open the kitchen door. Within a minute rain is dripping from my nose, along with snot and tears, and my bare legs are papered with wet, windblown leaves. Clint looks somewhat calmer outside, where other, less-alarming noises drown out the ones I am making.

Across the road is a hayfield, mowed into a giant spiral of golden stubble. It winds around to a flat-topped granite boulder at the center. I walk through the field, and the rough grass scratches my legs. The rock is a pedestal, a frame, an altar: a place to put something important. Clint's eyes shift from my face to the rock and back. At first I am afraid to do it. Then I lay the baby there, carefully, in a hollow on the top of the boulder. It holds him like a cradle. I don't want him to roll off and land with his soft cheeks in the brittle stubble of the field, to scrabble on his stomach until his face is torn and he breathes in dirt. I just want him *away*.

I watch him look up into the rain, twitching and blinking every time a drop hits his eyes. He never turns his head toward me. I walk away and leave him there on the rock, and I think I will die.

A small cry floats to me on the wind. Back in the yellow house, I sleep.

I WAKE UP and remember. Oh, God, how long has it been? How long has my baby been lying outside in the storm? I struggle out of the quilt, which has glued itself to my wet clothes and muddy shoes. The kitchen door is still open, and the rain has slowed. I stumble across gravel, over weeds and grass. The sky is violet, edging toward dusk. The leaves of the birches flicker in the wind. Alive, alive. Let him be alive.

What I see on the boulder is this: two curves of eyelashes against pale cheeks, lips the same purple as the sky, a blue-tinged arm escaped from its wet blanket. I whisper his name, then, "Please"— hardly a word, just a pinch of air. When I lift him in my arms, I feel a tiny, warm breath on my neck.

HEADLIGHTS SWEEP UP the hill and across the field. My husband's car turns in to our driveway.

There is no place to hide a soaking baby.

The adrenaline doesn't drive me to action. My legs are slow and heavy as cement. The front door is standing open, and John will walk in and see puddles of water and wet leaves on the kitchen floor; our bed, muddy and littered with weeds; and an empty crib. He may think at first that someone has stolen our beautiful, dark-eyed baby—*Who wouldn't want him?* John might say—and that I rushed out into the storm to save him at great peril to myself.

But that story will fall apart, and we will be left with the truth. Whatever way I tell it, it is the same. John stands at the open kitchen door.

I call, "Help! Help!" as I walk toward him. He lifts his arms. I think he is reaching out to take Clint from me, but he puts his arms around us both.

Laura Freudig lives with her husband and six children on the same Maine island where she grew up. She is a reformed multitasker, strong-coffee drinker, and the author of a children's book, *Halfway Wild*.

EDITOR'S NOTE

In "Without a Big One," JP Infante provides the reader with a glimpse at the impact of incarceration on black and brown families. This powerful short story also touches upon issues of love, poverty, education, and mental health, all through the lens of one young child in Washington Heights.

The narrator of this story is Ray Ray, a boy whose stepfather is "in school" for selling drugs. From the first read, the editors of *Kweli* were united in our love for this story, and the humanized family at the center of it, and every subsequent reading has been a gift.

Prison reform and prison abolition are receiving increased mainstream attention, from the work of Angela Davis to Jay-Z's newly created Reform Alliance. "Prisons are an obsolete institution," Angela Davis tells us, "because they exacerbate societal harms instead of fixing them." As readers, we see the harms done to the family at the center of "Without a Big One," and we can only hope it will be healed over time. Community intervention has its place. Cages do not. Infante's art helps to move us away from these cages and closer to a more just and equitable society.

Laura Pegram, Editor in Chief
Kweli Journal

WITHOUT A BIG ONE

JP Infante

1.

You've thought about jumping.

It's a cold winter night. You sit next to Queeny on your fire escape. The cars on the freeway come and go like waves. The lights from the George Washington Bridge reflect off the Hudson River like the shine in glassy eyes. The river is a giant bathtub without a ship or boat to save anyone who might be drowning.

Your babysitter, Nilda, says suicide is like killing someone, and if you were to survive jumping off the fire escape, the police would arrest you for attempted murder. If you do try killing yourself, you plan to live through it because suicide only works if you survive. Nilda laughed when you told her the attempt is meant to get people's attention. She laughed because it's true.

You feel the cold wind. Look at the buildings across the river in New Jersey. They are far apart with too much space in between. There's no space between you and Queeny because you both need the warmth.

They used to call you Minene, and, before that, Chungo, even though your birth certificate says another name. Your stepfather, who's been away at school for three months, calls you son. Son, get me the TV controller. Son, listen to your mother. Son, stop talking about your heart.

Your stepfather can draw you and your extra-small heart. Queeny asleep at your feet. He can draw anything and anybody. He knows everything about sports, anime, video games, comic books, and toys. He's the strongest man you've met and the only man who has ever kissed you. He has never lied. When he turned himself in to school you felt like crying, but didn't, because you've never seen him cry.

Mary gave birth to you. She calls you Minene or Ray and sometimes your stepfather's name by mistake. Mary doesn't hear it when you call her mom. She calls you Raymond when Queeny plays with her shoes or does poo in the house. Mary doesn't love Queeny like your stepfather does. Mary is younger than all of your friends' mothers. Mary looks young like your babysitter, but you know Nilda's younger because she's happier than your mother.

Sometimes you sleep with Mary in the bedroom. You like rubbing her hair on your nose. Sometimes the smell of shampoo and cigarettes makes you sleepy. Sometimes the mix keeps you up at night. You usually sleep on the sofa bed in the living room because of your bladder disease. Recently it's been hard to hold your piss at night.

Your new doctor says konnichiwa all the time. He said kids who drink soda wet the bed and Mary believed him. You don't trust this doctor because when you asked if he was Chinese, he pointed to a red circle at the center of a white rectangle and said, Japanese. Then he smiled at Mary.

One night you fell asleep with Mary in the bedroom and her snoring woke you around midnight. The TV showed old men talking about bladder disease. The next morning at the kitchen table, you told Mary about bladder disease. She was shuffling mail, knife in hand. She stopped, looked at the bowl in front of you, and said, Mentiroso, before cutting open a red envelope in one try. She usually doesn't speak Spanish so you didn't understand her. The way Mary pronounced that word made her a stranger.

That morning you realize the Chinese doctor was flirting with her. You make a mental note to tell your stepfather when he calls from school. He's only called a couple of times since he left because the apartment phone is always being cut off and there are never minutes on Mary's prepaid cell phone.

Your babysitter, Nilda, calls you Ray Ray. She loves Queeny. Nilda is taller than Mary and has a fat ass. Whenever you hug her, you touch it and she doesn't say anything. Nilda is in love with you. You don't tell her you know because she has a boyfriend. Every time Nilda sees you she laughs, but not at you. It's just she's embarrassed of being in love with someone your age. At night in bed you imagine kissing Nilda and licking her lips.

Nilda is smart and Nilda is beautiful and Nilda reads you stories with curse words and words you don't understand. She says you're mature. She says you should draw your own drawings instead of tracing. One day, Nilda told her friend with the huge boobs you'll be a heartbreaker. Her friend asked, Would you be my boyfriend? It took a while before you answered because you didn't want to hurt Nilda's feelings. You blurted out, It depends, and Nilda's friend laughed. Nilda barely giggled because she was jealous. That day you knew you had to make it up to her. So when Nilda asked for a drink you put ice in her ginger ale. And when you gave her the soda you saw her face through the glass and Nilda looked like she was made out of gold.

Nilda reminds you of your homeroom teacher, Mrs. Vicioso, because she doesn't paternize. Paternize is a word Nilda taught you.

When she caught you tracing your stepfather's sketches Mrs. Vicioso said, You can do better.

Your stepfather did a sketch of Big Ralph, the supermarket owner from New Jersey who is always eating. Anytime Ralph tells you something he ends it with, Know what I mean, Jellybean? Ralph is scary because he's bigger than that gorilla you saw in the zoo. His breathing sounds like he just climbed up the stairs even if he's been sitting in a chair. Sometimes while standing he nods off. It looks like he's gonna fall on his ass and never get up.

Nilda called Ralph a Glue-Ton once. She says the word comes from the Latinos in Greece and it means "to swallow." Nilda says Latino is a language that's dead because it killed itself or someone killed it. You're not sure how Latinos made it to Greece, but Mrs. Vicioso says they live all over the world because of Spain. You know the word means more than "to swallow." It has to do with someone who can't get enough of something, but you can't remember what Nilda said.

Ralph used to bring shopping bags full of food from his supermarket before your stepfather left for school. The fridge has been empty since then, and you haven't seen Ralph. You have seen Nilda's secret friend, Gregorio. You almost forget about him because Nilda said not to tell anyone he comes around. You don't like Gregorio because when he visited he only paid attention to Nilda. You went to trace your stepfather's drawings and fell asleep on the sofa.

2.

Today you wake up to the smell of piss and alcohol. Not the type the Chinese-Japanese wannabe doctor rubbed on you, but the one

Mary smells like. Did you wet the bed? Feel your underwear. Take them off. The faded Superman looks normal. Dry. Put your clothes on for school. Mary is not awake to make you shower.

Today is different. You won't walk the long way through boring Riverside Drive or climb up a mountain-hill to Fort Washington Avenue. Today you'll take the shortcut with your best friend, Frankie, even though your stepfather told you not to take the short way without him.

Frankie calls you Ray Ray like the rest of your classmates. When the two of you walk to school he talks nastier than a cockroach-filled radio. You two have always taken the long way because the shortcut goes under the George Washington Bridge through a pathway of broken glass and needles. Where zombies live. Frankie says zombies smoke crack. He knows all this because he has two older brothers. One is away at college, like your stepfather, and the other is in jail for having weed.

Frankie decides to wait after school to take the shortcut. After school you meet Frankie and follow him through Fort Washington Park. He ignores the other kids on the monkey bars and swings. You notice two empty swings, but Frankie doesn't stop. Ask yourself if you're scared. Are you scared? The thought of taking the shortcut without your stepfather makes you wanna pee. You pass the dog pen and wonder what Queeny's doing. Some dogs bark and others sniff around and the rest run in circles.

Frankie sits on a bench that faces New Jersey when you reach the back entrance of the park. He starts talking about two airplanes crashing into the George Washington Bridge and ends up talking about his brother calling from Rikers.

"Is he scared of jail?" you ask.

"Nope. It's only the skinny guys who get raped."

"Are you scared of taking the shortcut?"

Frankie doesn't answer. He kicks a diaper down the stairs.

You remember your house phone might be back on so you stand and exit the park. You rush down the stairs that lead to the freeway. Shattered glass crunches like cornflakes with each step. You almost slip on frozen garbage. You make it to the sidewalk next to the freeway and see a large brown box under the scaffolding between the George Washington Bridge and the buildings on Riverside Drive.

"There's a shoe coming out the box over there," says Frankie.

Pick up a plastic bottle. Throw it. The bottle bounces off and rolls down the cracked pavement. The shoe doesn't move.

"Shit, Ray Ray, he's dead," says Frankie.

Frankie and you collect whatever bottles and rocks aren't smeared with shit. Wait. 1 . . . 2 . . . 3 . . . Attack! Bottles shatter and rocks dent the box. Stop. The laughing ends and the hum of speeding vehicles on the freeway and the bridge return. The box stands still.

Walk on the sidewalk by the freeway. There's a path that diverges into the street that leads to your building on Riverside Drive. The cars pass fast and close to this narrow path so you walk under the scaffolds where the zombies live. The scaffolds are part of an abandoned construction next to the bridge. There are broken handrails, burnt benches, and dirt with cracked pavement. A zombie folds a garbage bag big enough for two bodies. He smiles at you.

"That crackhead keeps looking at us," says Frankie. The two of you turn around before walking any closer to the zombie with the giant garbage bag. You walk back the long way home. When you reach the stairs that lead to Fort Washington Park you notice there's no shoe coming out the brown box.

"He's not there cause he's alive," says Frankie.

"Let's see what's inside."

Pick up a bottle. Frankie is behind you. Glance at the stairs that lead to Fort Washington Park and the dog pen and your school and everything that's safe. Touch the cold cardboard. Listen. Meowing. Look through a hole while holding your nose. No cats. Turn around and a few feet away a zombie in a ripped black sweater has a rock in his hand. You freeze. Frankie runs up the stairs. The zombie throws the rock. You duck.

Frankie shouts from the top of the stairs. "He's got a knife!"

Worry. Hold the dirty glass bottle with both hands. The zombie walks like he's on a tightrope about to fall. The closer he gets, the more it smells like piss and the more you want to pee. You hear someone calling your name. Look up the stairs. Frankie's gone. Look over your shoulder. Feel the cold wind from the passing vehicles. Imagine your stepfather is watching, waiting to yell at you for taking the shortcut without him. Throw the bottle. It bounces off the zombie's chest. Run up the stairs and take the long way home.

A breeze of shit and piss blows out of the apartment when you push open the door. Mary whips Queeny with your stepfather's belt. Queeny runs to you whimpering with a trail of blood behind her. Every seven months she bleeds. Mary's eyes are swollen like she just woke up or finished crying. She isn't wearing any makeup. The darkness under her eyes looks like shadows. As Queeny trembles between your legs, you realize how ugly Mary's become.

"This dog is gone," yells Mary. "We're getting rid of it today."

Nausea. Hold your nose. All this could be easily cleaned: the drops of blood, the pieces of shoes, the chewed corners on the sofa, the rubbles of shit and the puddles of piss.

"Just clean it," you say.

Mary throws a shoe at you.

You duck and shout, "I hate you."

After hours of crying and threats of running away, you find yourself on Pinehurst Avenue close to where Olivia, a friend of your stepfather, lives. Queeny is on a leash ahead of you and Mary.

"Rich people live around here," says Mary. "They'll adopt her."

Drop the leash. Hope Olivia finds her. Follow Mary. Don't look back. Queeny follows you, dragging her metal leash over the concrete. So you end up in Fort Washington Park and leave Queeny in the dog pen, where she forgets about you and chases after the other dogs.

That night Mary asks if you want to sleep with her.

You say, "I hate you," and lick your lips, tasting the salt from tears and boogers.

"We can't afford that dog. She was starving," says Mary, slamming the bedroom door.

3.

Three days have passed and you haven't killed yourself. Your stepfather hasn't called. Frankie hasn't been to school since the day you attacked the zombie. Mrs. Vicioso says he's sick. You've asked the dog owners in Fort Washington Park about Queeny, but no one has seen a reddish brown dog with hazel eyes that looks like a bulldog but is really a mutt.

This morning Mary woke you up for school by caressing your face because she knows you're mad about Queeny. She caressed your face at the hospital after almost drowning in the bathtub. You saved her that day by pulling her head out the water and holding on tight to her hair.

After school you find Nilda sweeping the kitchen. Pass her and go to the living room. Sit on the sofa. Wait for her to say something. She says something. Ignore her. She drags the broom into the living room and stands under the lamp like an angel-witch with a glow over her head.

"I'm sorry about Queeny," she says.

"Queeny's dead."

"You're wrong, Ray. They adopt dogs like Queeny."

"Don't paternize me."

"What?"

"Don't paternize me."

"You mean patronize. Do you think I'm patronizing you?"

"Depends."

You go and sit at the kitchen table and look out the window. Think about jumping out.

Nilda throws words at you while cooking spaghetti because it's the only food left.

"Stroke," yells Nilda.

"It's like to strike, but only harder like a punch."

Stirring the pot, Nilda says, "Nope, it's a gentle touch like petting a cat."

"Didn't you say it was a heart attack?"

"Nope," she says with her back to you. "It's a soft touch. Next word . . . Independent."

"Being single and happy—"

There's a knock on the door. Think about your stepfather. Think about Queeny. Think about Nilda's secret friend, Gregorio. Nilda checks her cell. She turns a knob on the stove and walks out of the kitchen. Think about jumping out the window and breaking one leg.

"Come on, baby, she ain't gonna say shit," says the man in the hallway.

"I can't. It's my job," says Nilda.

"Come on, love."

"Only for a few minutes."

The door closes. Locks click. A man in a Yankee baseball hat extends his hand. Stare at it. He wears a leather jacket, jeans, and black boots. He's younger than your stepfather.

"Hi, Mr. Rodriguez," says the man.

"This is my friend, Nino," says Nilda.

"Yes, her boyfriend," says the man.

Your chest feels funny. Think about your heart murmur. Cavity. Nilda says anything can have a cavity, not only teeth.

"Daydreaming, Mr. Rodriguez?" asks the man with his hand out.

"Stop calling him that," says Nilda. "He's not in the mood."

Her friend, Nino, says he's seen you around. He says most stray dogs are adopted. Ignore him. Walk out of the kitchen with your plate.

You hear loud whispering in the kitchen.

"Are you seriously thinking of going?" asks Nino.

"I'm going," says Nilda. "It has nothing to do with Greg."

"What is it with you and this Greg guy?"

"Some of my friends are going to be male."

"I ain't bring Gregorio up. Why travel so far?"

"Because I want to," says Nilda in five hard whispers.

Dishes slam in the sink.

Wake up after falling asleep on the sofa. Water runs in the bathtub. Nino sits on the other end. A picture book and a jackknife rest on his lap.

"Mr. Rodriguez," says Nino, fixing his belt. "You think keeping a secret is important if it could get someone in trouble?"

Rub your eyes. Don't say anything.

"Would you get me in trouble, Mr. Rodriguez?"

You don't understand. Stay shut. He's a stranger.

"Have you ever gone under the bridge?" asks Nino.

"No."

"You sure you haven't gone under the scaffolds?"

"Yea . . . But with my stepfather. I can't go alone."

"If you snitch, Mr. Rodriguez—"

"Why you call me that?"

"Respect," says Nino. "Nilda says you hate being patron-ized . . . I'll get to the point. You ain't tell Nilda you saw me under the scaffolds because you ain't a snitch. If Nilda found out you saw me she'll think I was doing something wrong. And if I tell your mom I saw you throwing bottles at bums you'll get in trouble. But I ain't a snitch."

Nod because you almost understand. He thinks you saw him taking the shortcut under the bridge.

"You kept a secret. I trust you, Mr. Rodriguez."

Nino flips through the pages of *Where the Wild Things Are*. "Lonely boy surrounded by monsters. Sounds like *Beasts of No Nation*."

Nino doesn't look like someone who likes books. His hat is now to the back. He's like those guys with red eyes that lean with one foot against the wall and sit on milk crates by the corner. Guys like Frankie's drug-dealing brother.

"His mom sends him to bed without supper," says Nino.

"That book is for little kids," you tell him. "You know about heart murmurs?"

"Heart problem?" says Nino, scratching the few hairs on his chin.

"I have one. Mary says I was born with an extra-small heart."

"Who's Mary?"

"My mother."

"You look healthy. Nilda said you wanna run away."

"Sometimes."

"Me too," says Nino, "but I wanna run back to my parents' place."

"Why?"

"I got kicked out for selling . . . for . . . taking the shortcut."

"I haven't talked to my stepfather in mad long," you say.

"Reading helps you not think about people you miss. You gotta read a lot to be with a girl like Nilda."

Don't believe that Nino reads. He's not like Nilda.

"Imagine you had a girlfriend with a new friend named Gregorio," says Nino. "Now imagine this girlfriend mentions this new friend lent her a boring book called *School Days* by Patrick something. And your girlfriend says it's better than the book that you like, *Beasts of No Nation*."

"She thinks that other school-book is better than the beast-book?" you ask and try not to think about Nilda's secret friend.

"Yup, that's what Nilda thinks. She's never finished *Beasts of No Nation* cause it's too violent. I read it and loved it and I don't even like reading. I never finished *School Days* because it's boring. I wonder why she likes that boring book, *School Days*, so much."

"Because it's not violent?"

"No, no, wrong, Mr. Rodriguez. Remember this Gregorio friend told her about the *School Days* book." He starts cleaning his nails with the jackknife. "How would you feel if you finally read a book to impress your girl and she doesn't even read the book you read?"

"Jealous because she likes Gregorio's book better."

"Shit, you're smart. Has Nilda talked to you about Gregorio?"

"Nope," you say, rubbing your chest. Your heart hurts when you lie but would hurt even more if you snitch. "Is Nilda your girlfriend or your friend?"

"My girlfriend," he mumbles.

"Are you scared that Gregorio is bigger than you?"

Nino laughs. "I'm never scared. He might be taller but not bigger—"

Nilda comes out of the bathroom with her hair messed up. She asks for clean blankets. Nino puts one finger over his lips. You tell her the blankets are dirty. Go to the bedroom. Nilda makes the bed over with the same dirty sheet even though Mary had already made the bed that morning. When she's done you fall on the bed. Underneath one of the pillows is a moist spot that smells like Clorox. Fall asleep.

Fall with Mary. She holds your hand tight. There's a bridge in the sky above. The wind feels like a cold shower. Steam comes out of Mary's mouth because of the cold outside or something deep inside. The fall isn't so bad and it feels like a roller-coaster ride. As you plummet notice two objects falling below you. The two objects grow closer until you drop past them. Look up. See your stepfather and Queeny floating in the air. Both bodies disappear. You can't find Mary. Try flying. Feels like you're swimming. You're drowning. Swim.

Wake up and smell Queeny. The lamp reflects on the TV screen, where the only clean spot is your handprint in a thick layer of dust. The hamper teems with dirty clothes and a puddle of jeans around

it. Shades cover the two fire escape windows. Stretch your legs. It's
not Queeny you smell but your own piss. Mary will go mad when
she finds out.

Nilda could dry the bed with a blow-dryer. Ever since Nilda
surprised Mary with a visit she fixes everything. Nilda was dressed
in black slacks and a gray shirt. She wore makeup, her hair was
blow-dried, and an ID hung around her neck. Nilda wrote in a
black notebook and asked about you dialing 911 and saving Mary's
life when she almost drowned in the bathtub. At first Mary told you
not to tell Nilda anything because she was going to try to take you
away. But Nilda helped Mary get food stamps and a sofa bed and
babysits whenever Mary goes out.

If Nilda doesn't dry the bed Mary will go mad. Your jeans stick
to your legs. You almost shower, but change jeans instead. The living room is dim with the kitchen light. Nilda's gone. Mary snores
on the sofa like always. She probably forgot parent-teacher conference is tomorrow. Scratch your tear ducts. The crust goes in your
nails. The floor creaks. Bite your nails. Run away because she went
crazy the last time you wet the bed. Put your coat on. Look at Mary
dreaming before you leave. Grab her by the wrist and touch your
face with her hand. Her watch says 11:30 p.m. There's a hole in between her nostrils. She coughs and gasps for air. Press on her heart
like the ambulance man. She coughs. She doesn't open her eyes like
when you pulled her out of the bathtub.

Mary says, "Chris?" but doesn't wake up.

It's nighttime but Riverside Drive is not scary. It's not like morning when there are no parked cars. The yellow in the apartment
windows tells you who's awake. Sometimes you can see the shadows of families on walls and ceilings. You cross the empty streets
in the dark cold. The winds are angry on Pinehurst Avenue. Stop

coughing. You can't. Keep coughing. Boogers run down your stuffy nose. Wish you had a hole between your nostrils like Mary.

Surprise! Ralph is in front of Olivia's building. The fat guy from New Jersey who used to bring food to your house, but disappeared when your stepfather left to school. He sits on the stoop with shopping bags. He is nodding off like a zombie. But Ralph is too fat to be a zombie. If Ralph sees you he'll snitch and tell your stepfather. Run back home.

Run up your building's stairs. Hope your stepfather hasn't called.

Mary blocks the door to the apartment. "Where have you been?"

"Nowhere."

"Want me to tell Chris you ran away because you wet the bed?"

The cuticles on your middle finger bother you. Bite them off. It burns. "I saw Ralph taking food to Olivia's building."

"What?" asks Mary. "Big Ralph?"

"Yeah."

"Let's go," she says.

When you and Mary get to Pinehurst Avenue she tells you to stay across the street from Olivia's building. She leaves you her cell phone and tells you to call the cops if anything happens. Mary enters Olivia's building. Wish Ralph was taking food to your house. Think about how the lightposts glow the color of pee. Look at the moon. It doesn't look like it's made out of cheese.

Mary runs out of Olivia's building with two shopping bags. "Let's go," she says. "Let me get the phone."

Keep up with Mary as she talks on the cell.

"Answering machine, Ralph? You fat piece of shit. If I find you in the Heights buying from that cutthroat, Olivia, I'm gonna make

Chris cut your balls off when he comes out. I could've gotten you what you needed like Chris used to but you go behind my back to Olivia . . ."

"Why you mad at Ralph?"

"He's a drug addict," she says. "I don't want you around junkies."

The next morning you wake up alone in the bedroom. Mary didn't wake you up for school but she never does. You hear a man in the living room. Think about your stepfather.

Nino is on the sofa, talking on his cell.

"I won't throw it in your face. I'm doing the boy a favor, not you . . . Studying abroad ain't about studying. People travel to fuck." Nino sees you, puts one finger on his lips, and hangs up.

"Is Mary in the hospital?"

"No, your mom's running errands and Nilda's at work."

"I'm late for school."

"You won't miss nothing. It's a half day today. Don't tell Nilda I let you stay home . . . Hungry? I ordered Chinese for breakfast."

"It's half a day because it's parent-teacher conference today."

"I know," he says. "Nilda and your mom won't be back until later so I'm gonna take you."

Around dusk you and Nino take the shortcut to school. One of the zombies yells from under the scaffolds, "Arturo!"

Nino throws a hand in the air and says, "Dry."

When you reach the foot of the stairs that lead to Fort Washington Park, you ask Nino, "Why does Nilda help my family?"

"It's her job. Plus, you remind her of her cousin Juan."

"Does Juan have a dog?"

"Nope."

"Did Juan get left back?"

"I don't know. Maybe. Community college is like being left back."

"Was Juan born with a heart murmur?"

"I'm not sure, Mr. Rodriguez."

"Did Juan's mother try to suicide herself?"

"Juan's mother died from taking drugs," says Nino, cleaning his nails with the jackknife.

The moon is out when you reach an empty Fort Washington Park. No runaway kids on the playground or runaway dogs in the dog pen. The swings are so still they look frozen. You can see right through the monkey bars. There's no line for the big slide. Nino and you sit on a bench by the water fountain because you're early. There are no stars, just an airplane's red light in the sky.

"Nilda said she's going to Spain."

"I know." Nino opens his eyes wide like they need air.

"You sell drugs?"

"I know people in jail for selling drugs," says Nino.

"That bum called you Arturo. You got different names for different people?"

"Yup, and different secrets," says Nino. "Mr. Rodriguez, if you knew Nilda had another boyfriend, would you tell me?"

"Depends."

When you enter the school Nino drops you off in the gym where there are no adults and leaves to talk to Mrs. Vicioso. There are big kids throwing basketballs at smaller kids and boys and girls under the bleachers. A girl in a pink coat chokes a girl in a blue coat. A boy runs up to you, screams, and then runs away, leaving a sneaker behind. Two boys howl at the ceiling lights.

You sit on the bleachers, ignoring the kissing sounds below you and watching everyone's parents drop them off. Frankie enters the gym with his father. His father looks old and stupid because he doesn't know English. Frankie is a liar who abandoned you. Your stepfather would kill Frankie's father in a fight. Frankie's father doesn't care about Frankie, because he leaves him behind with all these crazy kids in the gym. Frankie runs across the gym and the closer he gets, the more he looks like his father.

"I spoke to my brother," says Frankie. "He's not in Rikers. He's in the SHOCK program. Like a boot-camp jail. He saw your father. There's this drill sergeant with a tattoo on his arm of a black baby hanging on a rope that makes them do push-ups—"

"He ain't my father. He's my stepfather and he's in college."

"It's not a real college like my other brother is in. They just let them take a test for a diploma."

"Stop lying."

You punch Frankie in the face. He walks backward, crying like a little bitch. Frankie covers his nose with blood dripping between his fingers. He might bleed to death. A crowd forms around the two of you. Run to the back exit. Hurry!

Run across the street to an empty Fort Washington Park. The police will arrest you. Think about drowning in the Hudson River. Run downstairs to the freeway. Pause at the foot of the stairs. On the other side of the eight lanes of freeway is another park and after that is the Hudson River. Think before crossing. Feel the wind of the cars speeding by like they're racing.

Someone grabs your arm. Scream.

"Give me money."

"I don't got nothing."

The zombie puts you in a headlock and presses cold metal on your throat. He searches your pockets. "I'll rip your heart out."

"I was born with a heart murmur."

Close your eyes. Pray to your stepfather. The zombie flies off you. Nino slams the zombie on the ground. He jumps on the zombie, chokes him with one hand and holds his jackknife with the other.

"Don't stab the zombie, Nino."

Nino looks at you. He looks at the zombie before letting him go. While on your way home Nino's cell rings.

"Yes, he was in the park," he says. "His mother will call you."

Nino doesn't ask why you punched Frankie.

"Let's make a deal, Mr. Rodriguez. If you don't let Nilda leave to Spain I promise not to tell anyone about tonight. Deal?"

"Okay, but tell me . . . is my stepfather in jail for selling drugs?"

"Yeah, Raymond," says Nino, and he pats your head. "I'm sorry."

Believe Nino. Your stepfather is in jail. You don't want to snitch on Nilda but you'd rather be a snitch than hide something from Nino. So you tell him about Gregorio.

"Mr. Rodriguez, you don't gotta pretend you know Nilda's friend. I won't tell anyone about tonight regardless."

Don't tell Nino anything else about Gregorio because it hurts his feelings. He doesn't believe you because he doesn't want to believe.

The next morning Mary's snoring wakes you in the bedroom. It's Saturday but you don't feel like watching cartoons. On one window the shade is halfway down so you see the dust the sun brings. On the other window the shade is fully drawn so there's no dust. It's better to keep the blinds down because the dust makes you sneeze.

Mary's cell phone vibrates on the floor.

"Hello?"

"Will you accept the collect call from Christian Ruiz?" asks a robotic voice.

"Yes."

"Hello," says a raspy voice.

It sounds like your stepfather is crying. Stay shut. Listen.

"I'm sorry I haven't called," he says. "I didn't want to—"

"Nilda says men cry. You know Queeny is gone?"

"I heard. Is Nilda that Children Services woman?"

"Yeah. She helped Mary get a job but Mary got sick and lost it."

Your stepfather coughs. "If she's sleeping give her a kiss."

Rub your nose against Mary's and smell cigarettes. Love the smell. Remember how she used to laugh with a cigarette in her mouth, one eye squinting because of the smoke. Touch her lips. The dryness feels like torn plastic. Lick your mother's lips.

"Are you drawing?" he asks.

"Yeah, tracing yours."

"You can't trace my drawings or take the shortcut."

"Are you in jail for selling drugs?"

He clears his throat. "Son, I told you I'm in school."

And even though Frankie, Nino, and the voice inside you all say that your stepfather is in jail, you decide to believe your stepfather.

———————

JP Infante is a teacher and writer who curates and hosts arts and culture events. He has taught creative writing at the City University of New York's Lehman College and writing workshops throughout New York City. He holds an MFA in fiction from the New School. Through the "JP

Infante in Conversation" series, he hosts talks with poets and writers. He is a contributing editor for *Dominican Writers*.

His fiction, nonfiction, and poetry can be found in *Kweli Journal, The Poetry Project, Uptown Collective, Dominican Writers, POST(blank)* magazine, *The Manhattan Times*, and other publications. His writing has won the Bernard L. Einbond Memorial Prize, the Aaron Hochberg Family Award, *DTM* magazine's "Latino Identity in the U.S." essay contest, and other awards.

EDITORS' NOTE

In Tamiko Beyer's "Last Days 1," literature and poetry become, for a few revolutionaries, "a system of belief, a way to navigate the dissolving world." For the world, during these "last days of empire," is indeed dissolving, into a mélange of "synthesized laughter" and "canned sounds" pushed by corporate omnipresence.

With each read, we are taken by this story's vision of the future and what it reflects of the present. This is more than an apocalypse story—it is composite and collage, a new way of storytelling that blurs all lines between poem and prose and essay. This is unnerving in the way genre-bending work should be. It reflects and refracts the end of the world.

Yet there is love—real love, queer love—at the center, and it is the presence of this love that stands as a stark marker of resistance in the face of our modern future-present: drone-based surveillance, emptied libraries, vacated culture. Beyer connects us to these rebel poets, and she reminds us that there was once a world where literature and love flourished. She reminds us that we can make that world again.

Chase Burke, Fiction Editor
Cat Ingrid Leeches, Editor
Black Warrior Review

LAST DAYS 1

Tamiko Beyer

"Safe is an interpretation"
—Kate Greenstreet, *Young Tambling*

WE DIDN'T EXPECT the eagerness that filled us on the last days of empire. For what, we couldn't exactly say.

Metal glistened on the streets in the hot September days. The sun no longer a dandelion; the sun most definitely a muzzle. When it set, the Corporation—keen to kill the dark—flipped the switch.

Then, the marble facades of buildings were suddenly up-lit, street-lights swirled incandescent, and thousands of people hurtled through the furnace of synthesized laughter, pop songs, and an unlimited desire for all.

Some of us were on the edges, blocking out the canned sounds and lights as best we could. Building something new, something old. We could feel the northern half of our planet begin to tilt away from the sun.

I am on the cusp of change, and the curve is shifting fast.

It was an experience and then it was a memory. And then a system of belief, a way to navigate the dissolving world.

I wanted to become more salt-wind, less reflection. To become quiet enough to hear the ancestors.

ANCESTORCHORUS

Find the source at the underwater
roots, at the mudline:
fragile strands of a new language
among cattails and seed casings.
Trust the fibers
will lean in the right direction,
will not mislead you.

Child, we have always laid
one strand over, then under the next,
over and under, over and under—
until something like true
meaning emerges from the twist
of our fingers. This basket
is for you: an exhortation, a map.
Soon you will need to reach
all of us in this river of time
with the truest sentences
you can weave.

There were five of us in that small apartment, hauling water, coding and decoding, soldering metal, constructing strategies, drafting poems. I lifted heavy objects and learned to stitch up an open wound.

I no longer thought of myself as a girl. I was often afraid. At the same time, I glistened in the everyday fever brought on by Wave's eyes opening, the morning sky breaking.

When we met, Wave said holding on was dangerous. The taste of hope could make us reckless. I knew what she meant, but despite ourselves, I came to love how she tasted more than I loved any fruit on my tongue.

ANCESTORCHORUS

Light breaks the glass
separating you
from the present.
The dangerous words
chime in the wind, spike
into sand and grass.
Behold the other kind of blade:
power of seed
turned blossom, turned fruit.

In the afternoons we would cross the river on the train, skimming ancient tracks into the center of the city where things were bought and sold on a grand scale. We slid into the gaps of commerce, knowing *all warfare is based on deception.*

So many people were building scaffolding against crumbling structures, using incantations from their fathers as mortar.

But some attempted to excavate the signals buried deep within their bodies; some tried to listen to their heartbeats.

Those were the ones we were looking for. We slipped them a scrap of paper, then dissolved back into the crowd.

ANCESTORCHORUS

Words can obscure like clouds
or reveal like the tidal pull.
Do you remember rain?

*The state of emergency is also always
the state of emergence.* Where does the water go
when ocean draws out its lowest tide?

When the new recruits followed the poem to find us, we put them to work or gave them maps to others in need of their skills. We were hundreds of loose groups across the country, fashioning transformation out of starlight and strategy, spindrift and solidarity.

I was impatient for the waking, the sharp sensation of light and promise. I thought I understood.

But there was still so much to learn. Wave reminded me of the libraries they had shut down decades ago, their floors like silk, books heavy with promise. That's where we went: picking the locks, scraping away the dust, memorizing what we could.

Power grids, water-sewer lines, and fiber optic cables snaked their way across the city. We became deft in mapping and coordinates, diversion and distraction. We discovered the patterns the Corporation relied on, found the back doors, planted the traps with care.

Creating new economies in the heart of capital required cunning and poetic imagination. We knew we were being watched when the NICE drones paused above our fire escape.

But cooking and dancing were not yet crimes. We could plan just as well stirring the pot in three-four time as in stillness around the kitchen table.

The patience is in the living. Time opens out to you. We hummed and we sang. We simmered soup and kneaded flour and water. We mapped out the next tactics.

Notes

"I am on the cusp of change, and the curve is shifting fast."
—Audre Lorde, "A Burst of Light"

"All warfare is based on deception."
—Sun Tzu, *The Art of War*

". . . the state of emergency is also always the state of emergence."
—Homi Bhabha, 1986 foreword to Frantz Fanon's *Black Skin,
White Masks*

"The patience is in the living. Time opens out to you."
—Claudia Rankine, *Citizen*

———————

Tamiko Beyer is the author of *Last Days*, forthcoming in 2021; *We Come
Elemental*; and two chapbooks of poems. Her work has been published in
*Black Warrior Review, Denver Quarterly, The Georgia Review, Literary Hub,
The Rumpus, Hyphen, Dusie,* and elsewhere. She has received grants,
fellowships, and residencies from Kundiman, Hedgebrook, and the
Astraea Lesbian Writers Fund, among others. A social justice communi-
cations writer and strategist, she spends her days writing truth to power.
She lives in Dorchester, Massachusetts, and online at tamikobeyer.com.

EDITORS' NOTE

We selected "Good Hope" by Enyeribe Ibegwam for publication in the Spring/Summer 2018 issue of *Auburn Avenue* because of its enthralling portrayal of Nigerian Americans navigating life in the United States. It fit perfectly within our issue's theme, "The American Story, A.D. 2018," and gave attention to the complex—and often misunderstood—immigrant experience.

In the story, a nephew confronts and takes stock of his estranged uncle's life. These characters' lives are split and reconvened and woven together in a way that shows each of their disappointments and, at the same time, their shared joys. Ibegwam questions where home is and the beauty and tragedies that live there. The narrative holds up a mirror to its characters, and its readers, and asks them describe all that they see.

Chuck Huru, Editor in Chief
Matthew B. Kelley, Fiction Editor, Spring/Summer 2018
Auburn Avenue

GOOD HOPE

Enyeribe Ibegwam

1.

"What are we eating tonight?" JV asked, scratching his bearded chin. "You know I came to stay."

He was talking to my big sister, Uzumma. He was our mother's older brother, our uncle, although we called him JV. There was never a time he wanted to be called Uncle—none of that respect-for-elder procedure with him.

"My boy," he would say to me, "does *Uncle* put any money in my bank account?"

When I say I only knew that the J in his initials was for Joachim, nothing about the V, people flinch at me as though I have no front teeth. "Call me JV," he said, his voice honed by years of smoking Benson & Hedges. There must have been a time when he was called by his name, and not by initials.

Back then, all I wanted to do was assure him that there was nothing wrong with living like a teenager. What was wrong about living in my parents' house, with no job or personal responsibility? I never wanted him to feel shame for himself, even though I was ashamed.

"Sure, this is our house, you can eat whatever you like," Uzumma answered him. I just wish she had hidden the sarcasm in her voice. I saw it as her eyes lit up. Covering her mouth with her right palm, she controlled her giggles at his retreating back. He turned, tossed M&Ms at me, and said I could give Uzumma some, if I felt like it.

It didn't take much to entice Uzumma and me in those days. Painted sepulcher, as my father used to refer to things he had no interest in. And if there was something JV had mastered, it was lavishing us with treats. Chocolate bars, wafers, cone ice cream, éclairs, colored popcorns, meat pies, and scotch eggs.

JV CAME TO live with us the Easter Sunday of my seventh birthday; it would be four years later that I started having hair on my armpits. Not thick black hair, but hair anyway. From my earliest memory of him moving into our house, my father never seemed interested in him. My father and JV merely tolerated each other, or really they never liked each other. Back in the days, before my parents got married, JV had said my father was no good for my mother.

Years earlier my father had used lyrics from Rex Lawson's "Love Mu Adure" to serenade my mother. When all he had was his engineering degree, which fetched him a job teaching mathematics at the community secondary school in Emekuku while my mother was running her housemanship at the Federal Medical Center in Owerri. All that was a long time ago, maybe three years before Uzumma, who is two years older than me, was born. If family ground-talks are something to go by, JV was just looking out so his sister—my mother—wouldn't marry a low-life engineer. But family hearsay also insisted JV had no means of livelihood after graduating from university years before his medical doctor sister, and that he still squeezed money from her. But this is about JV and me, not about JV and them.

IN THOSE YEARS when he still lived with us, he idled at home all day and stepped out in the evenings when my parents returned from work, so he could play draught, drink beer, and eat peppered snails with the allowance my mother gave him every week.

"Of what use is a rich in-law?" he always asked his drinking buddies in his tipsy state that made his voice rumble. It was in one of his rumbling-voiced moments one night that he announced to my parents that he wanted to go to America. It must have been a Friday, because Uzumma and I were still up watching reruns of *The Jeffersons*, those episodes that our parents considered age-appropriate for us. He wanted to study at the University of Mississippi, he said. A friend of his already studying there had been sending him pictures and catalogues.

My mother rolled her eyes and sighed.

"But come to think of it, is it reasonable to school in the American South?" my father said, to no one in particular.

"Ole Miss is the Harvard of the American South," JV said. It sounded like something he had memorized with great care. In my life, I cannot remember a day that JV kept a job, and there he was, looking my parents in the face, between alcohol belches, insisting he wanted them to fund his American dream.

Many years later, I would have a chilling recollection of my mother's face that Friday night as JV addressed her and my father in the dining area of my parents' house in Aladinma Estate. The way my mother pursed her lips, how her eyes became solid beads as she nodded yes in agreement with JV. A lie so good that JV believed it, even though I saw it for what it was. My father was, and still is, a man of few words; he didn't say much that night, beyond small suggestions. He looked at my mother through the top gaze of his reading glasses as though it were she he was speaking to. For some childish reason, Uzumma and I pretended we couldn't hear what they were discussing, even though in years to come we had our annoying cousin, Dominic, play the role of JV as we reenacted that scene until we were so good we could have won acting awards for our performances.

JV stopped speaking to both my parents and lived as though he were a tenant in our house. So my father agreed to sponsor his brother-in-law. I learned about this when I listened in on my father telling my mother that all JV was doing was guilt-treating her. Need I tell you that JV traveled that year? To America, not England, where my father had suggested was better for him. My father, already a senior engineer with Shell Exploration Company, put his joined fingers to his lips and coughed out $7,500 for JV's entire tuition and upkeep, which back in '81 was little competition to the naira. I remember the night he left.

PEOPLE WERE STILL allowed to accompany passengers past customs and straight to the boarding airplane. (Sounds impossible now, right?) Anyway, that night Uzumma cried herself to a vomit. I couldn't make sense of it: Why did she have to make Mommy run around, looking for a sink to rinse her mouth and wash her face, napkins to dry her up? Uzumma cried about how she was going to miss him, how the house would be boring without JV. I watched her in mild irritation. Did Mommy really deserve the stares the airport workers gave for bringing what looked like a sick child to the airport? I tried to distance myself, as though I weren't part of their party. I inherited from my father this tendency, as I did his brown eyes. It's the same disinterest I feel toward the evening news these days; I never watch it, because it starves me of knowledge.

As we exchanged hugs, JV promised to always remember us and said that we shouldn't forget him. I was the only one he gave a kiss on the forehead, and then he whispered into my ears.

"If you wait for me, I will come for you. Just be a good boy. JV will come back for you."

I looked him full in the face; he tried to conceal his expression, which showed the uncertainty his life was to take. Truth be told, he looked like a cornered house rat. Yes, a frightened rat, as he boarded that airplane headed for New York. From there he would find his way to Jackson and finally to Oxford, Mississippi.

2.

JV did keep in touch in those early years while he studied for an MBA. He wrote letters and sent postcards. In the beginning, he complained about Mississippi. His professors didn't want him there, a letter I found in my mother's drawer revealed, although his claim was one he couldn't back up.

"Can you believe that where I live," he wrote in another letter, "they don't sell ordinary alcohol on Sunday?" He wanted to leave and continue school in Washington, D.C., but it wasn't because of the alcohol thing, he insisted. My father would have none of his tales. "He chose to go there and started there; he must finish there."

He must have settled into that kind of living, because those complaints ceased. On one of the two family vacations when we visited

New York, my mother tried to contact him, but he never responded. It was during these visits that it started to dawn on me that most of the black people I saw in America were nothing like the Jeffersons or the Huxtables, who were from a new sitcom that year.

When my father was conferred the *Okaa Omee 1* of Emekuku and my mother the *Ugo Nwa Chinamere*, I expected JV to surprise me by coming. I can't explain why I hoped so much. I was an acne-faced teenager by then, and there was a girl I was infatuated with at school, but what I still remember are the shirtless drummers, their bodies glistening with sweat. I watched closely as the masquerades danced at the ceremony; one was about the height of JV. I watched the way its ankle swerved with rhythm, the twist and turns of its arms, as though I expected some act of trickery that would make the occupant take off the costume and reveal JV. Of course, that never happened; JV did not attend my parents' chieftaincy celebration.

He used to call us when we had a land phone. My mother was the one who took it upon herself to ask him to visit home. Then his calls ceased, and he never answered ours. He must have graduated, because I remember seeing a picture of him in his graduation robe. There was the story my mother told her friend, that he had taken up teaching at a community college, but maybe she was lying. During his span of being incommunicado, we were handed down tales about him. A community college professor in Tennessee, a contract worker for the South Carolina state government, a door-to-door insurance salesman in Atlanta, Georgia, then a job working with a lawn-mowing company in Houston, Texas; he was a supervisor at Walmart in Baltimore, Maryland; he drove trucks for a furniture company in Washington, D.C. With these stories, our hearts broke many times over—except, of course, my father's.

"They say he was seen sweat-soaked at the Million Man March in Washington, D.C.," my mother said, almost in tears one evening as we watched the news. JV turned fifty in Washington, D.C., doing whatever odd job it was he was doing in that populated American city. He was married, we heard. No, he wasn't; he just had a domestic partner—whatever that meant. Then he was divorced, then remarried, then divorced again. We set out to forget him. It was easy. We never mentioned his name and tried hard never to mention America, though the latter was impossible, seeing how America put itself in every television screen.

3.

I didn't see JV until I began living in Houston, Texas, as a thirty-year-old. I had two master's degrees from England and had worked for a few years at British Petroleum in London before I was transferred. From Texas, I found my way to D.C.

In D.C. it wasn't long before I looked JV up. My curiosity was kite-high. I heard from a family friend that he lived in the northeastern part of the city. But when I reached out to my few Nigerian connections, they mostly shook their heads, as though that explained his lot. No one really knew where he was.

"It was around the time taxi drivers were being killed all around D.C. that I stopped seeing JV ride his taxi," a woman, also from Emekuku like me, informed me. She thought she meant well. Before then, I never knew that JV drove taxis for a living.

I hired a private investigator, and it didn't take long before he found out the specifics of JV's existence.

"Anacostia *kwa?*" a man I called Uncle Aloysius out of civility enunciated over the phone when I informed him of the findings. "Do you really want to go there? The only good thing there is the name of a neighborhood. Good Hope Road is what they call it."

For days afterward, I thought about all the warnings I heard, from just about everyone I spoke to, about going to Southeast, as I stared at JV's address on my phone.

I GOT ON the Metro, plowed through morning commuters: stiff-looking men in solid-color suits and their briefcases. Women in business-style high heels, with bold-colored lipsticks and impatience in every stride. I stopped at the train station nearest to his house and got into a taxi. We drove past dozens of houses, some three-storied, others one, most two-storied, all painted in gloomy colors. Grayish reddish brown or glazed clay. Variety was limited. The pedestrians moved with an apprehension; they seemed burdened by the knowledge of what they had become. I thought about my childhood in Aladinma. When we returned from our holidays in New York, some of the children from another neighborhood would beg Uzumma and me to tell them about America. They wanted us never to exhaust our American stories, to pinch at our mountain of stories. How much they, even as children, idealized America. If only they knew then what they know now. Most of them, like me, have left home. Some to live in countries whose names they had never heard previously, countries so cold their ears numb in the winter. In places that promise yet fail them in many things many times over, they continue to stay. We like and comment on each other's pictures on Facebook. When we Skype each other, we talk about small things: how the government back home has failed, how home is only good for retirement. Never do we talk about our lives.

Never do we look each other long enough in the eyes; perhaps the mirrors there will only show us ourselves, the selves that we left at home. As the saying goes: to travel is to see.

PEOPLE WALKED PAST as though they had all the time in the world, yet in their feet was the calculating agility of a cat. The private investigator said that on the building where JV lived, the words LOVE YOUR BLACK NATION were written in orange graffiti.

The old three-story brownstone on Third Street in Southeast D.C. was nondescript, like a park bench: unworthy of a second glance. The only things that attracted a glance from me were the fluttering pigeons that homed in the dark spaces under the eaves of the brownstone next to his. A man the complexion of ginger-clove stood by the steps of the brownstone blowing cigarette smoke upward, his tattooed neck bared for me to see. He noticed me approaching, studied me swiftly, as if to see what trouble I would be, calculated that in my button-down long-sleeve shirt and blue jeans I was no threat, then hitched up his droopy jeans and grabbed his crotch. I swept past the porch and into the hallway. It smelled of wet dog and fried onions and soap. A teenage girl with flowing multicolor hair, wearing black harem trousers and a yellow top that bared her midriff, raced up the stairs behind me and stopped to flash me a letter. Before I could look at it, she screamed, "I got accepted," and continued past me, tears slick on her brown face.

THAT MORNING I'D had no mental picture of what JV would look like, but the girl's vanilla scent took me back to the tint of vanilla in JV's shaving powder.

I recalled JV in the backyard of our Aladinma house—back when houses in Aladinma still had just flower hedges and wire fences demarcating them—sitting on a fold-up chair and humming Jim Reeves's "A Railroad Bum." His lips curled as he sang.

I never seemed to have a dime, but I had myself a ball
Singing hi le hi lo, he li le li lo
I used to be a railroad bum but I'm not anymore

Thinking about that song still gives me the shivers these days. Maybe it's the lyrics about a once-upon-a-time drifter, or the vision the song conceives, not of Jim Reeves but of JV, in shorts and shirtless, soft-tapping his feet in glee, his beard fully covered in vanilla-scented shaving paste as my mother hands him his weekly allowance. That vision of him still visits me. Sometimes it's as clear as water; other times the water is rippled, and his image fragmented.

AFTER MULTIPLE KNOCKS, I sensed a presence on the other side of the door; someone was watching me from the peephole. I heard the click and jangle of locks. The person that opened the door of the apartment was far from my wildest imaginings of what JV would look like.

In the crack that the door chain allowed, his eyes narrowed in on me. "Kemoye?" he said, as if making sure I hadn't appeared there by some trick.

I stood dumbfounded.

He called my name again. "Kemoye." I could see the film of tears in his eyes.

I have had quite a few disappointments in my life. My friends have betrayed me; my secrets have been revealed; people have made promises they couldn't keep; I have had unfaithful girlfriends and disappointing jobs. None could compare to seeing JV.

They say that black doesn't crack, but if you have seen poverty, then you need a different saying.

When I greeted him, a disbelieving light appeared in his eyes.

"Your cheeks are an evidence of good living," his Aladinma friends used to say. If only they could see how hollow and shrunken those cheeks were now. The edges of his eyes and mouth crinkled, and his tired skin bore evidence to years of hard living. Those lips had been battered by smoking, and his hair had faded to the color of cigarette ash. But I couldn't tell what brand of cigarettes this brown bag of a man smoked; he smelled of lavender soap.

The room he led me to was cramped and small. Jimi Hendrix's poster was big on the wall, the bed was high and fluffy, and beside it sat a worn caramel velvet loveseat facing a striped armchair and a coffee table with Edward P. Jones's *All Aunt Hagar's Children* opened facedown.

How was I to begin a conversation with someone I hadn't seen in over twenty years? Our conversation treaded within the space of civility. I asked questions and tried to fill the awkward pauses with casual phrases and gestures that masked my disappointment. But in between I was focusing on his facial expressions. I watched him with a child's wonder, checking for signs of the JV I knew; his periodic humming, his sweet-talking and larger-than-life attitude.

"It's a tight country," he said, his voice naked as if from a not-distant memory.

He removed the cluster of clothes from the backrest of his armchair to make space so he could lean back. I called the cabdriver and asked him to be back in thirty minutes.

I knew what he wanted to say before he spoke. "Let the cab go. We will find our way. This place isn't as bad as some people make it seem. We virtually live behind the president."

I called the cabdriver back before I thought about what I was doing. I looked around the room: the ashtray with cigarette stubs by the window, the clothes tossed around, the harsh scent of tobacco and air freshener that hung in the air.

He started, "It's a country of ambitions, but it's hard." He grunted, spat into a paper towel, folded it, and continued. "Don't get me wrong, there are opportunities; I have seen plenty. Yet no matter how promising they are, once I try, they start to fizzle out. It's almost like trying to grip air. It amounts to nothing." He finished with his shoulders slouched, head bowed as he poured himself and me a glass of cheap liquor.

I wanted to counter him, to tell him that it was never too late.

He must have seen the rebellion in my eyes, because he silenced me with questions. "Do you know how many times I have tried? You think it's me? Then ask my roommate." There was no joy in his voice.

It was one of those slow-motion moments of life, where anything could happen. Love could triumph, or hate solidify. I watched JV cry. I was quiet because I saw what he thought of himself: a failure twice over.

"You were raised preppy, nothing wrong with that, but here we are like dry bones in the valley. In time you will realize this."

Never had I felt so slapped in my life. I wanted to tell him that I too had come upon that realization; that once, during a Christmas party at work, my boss, already tipsy, had nudged me and said, "Kemoye, you mean to tell me that you cannot dance? Dude, even the president can do the dougie." Beneath the nervous smile, I saw the flick of disappointment in my boss's eyes. Beyond awkward side-to-side movement, I couldn't dance as was expected of a black person. I wanted to tell him of an acquaintance who watched me rub my itchy nose and asked whether my drugs had finished. But I knew that those moments were small compared to what JV was living. I wanted to comfort him, to give something impossible to give his sixtyish self. I wanted to give him certainty as one would a child.

He went on about his chain of failed marriages, a son in military training—the only redemption that could keep him off the streets. There was a daughter on a scholarship at Juilliard, and another daughter, a teenager living with her own mother. He hadn't remarried and for years now had treated women with varying degrees of disinterest.

"I have long stopped suffering my heart. Bu . . . but . . ." JV continued, searching the ceiling for words. "Anyway, my life hasn't been a complete hell. I have been lucky enough to be black on a Saturday night." His words sank into me. *Lucky to be black on a Saturday night.* I must have read that somewhere.

"How about moving back to Nigeria? You can always start a business or teach at the university."

He looked at me as though I were a stranger.

"This is my country now; I'm my own progenitor. I'm here now." His voice seemed to come out of nowhere. "But if you hope to go back, start planning your exit now. Or else this place will sink its teeth into you, and then going back home will be impossible. Then you will realize that the place you left as home is no more, and instead all that is left is that which is inside you. Within you, you carry your own home."

———

WE TALKED AND talked that whole day. I didn't even realize when we both finished the bottle of liquor. I wondered what he did for a living. Did he still drive a taxi?

By early evening we had nothing left to ask each other. I thought I had scanned through all his photo albums, but my eyes caught something under his coffee table, in between thick books. It was an album I hadn't gone through. I flipped through it. The first photo was of me in a blue denim pinafore and green shirt holding a small plastic green samurai sword. My teeth flashed in a smile at the camera. Tucked between the photo and its transparent protective cover were these words: *Favorite nephew in the world.* He wrote in cursive. *Looks just like me, could have as well been my son.*

I continued flipping through. All the photos were of me. Some were of us and some even pictures of me as an adult, which he must have found on the internet. Something felt crushed inside me. I knew he was fond of me as a boy, and I always thought it was because everyone said I looked like him. The same clear umber complexion. How was I to know that he saw me as his son? I wondered why he never wrote to me all these years, why he had never tried to keep a relationship going with me.

I remembered what he said to me at the airport when he kissed me on the forehead—that he would come back for me. But JV had missed my childhood; I had grown up while waiting for him to fulfill his promise.

"I wrote personal letters to you," he said, "but you never wrote back. Maybe your mother never wanted you to see them."

I said nothing. It's an eerie realization, that two quiet people like us were better off quiet alone, not asking questions, pretending as if all those absent years never happened.

"You still like peppery chicken, right?" His voice boomed from the kitchenette.

"Sure."

I heard the clanks of knives and spoons. There was the harsh aroma of onions being sliced, and my eyes started to water. The aroma of sliced onions would be the perfect excuse if JV had seen my tears.

"Out of peppers. I better go buy some," he said. My eyes must have shown my protest, because he added, "You know you will spend the night with me, mister."

I nodded a yes; there I sat, a child to him again.

"Will you move with me to Texas?" I asked. It felt like the right thing to ask. To show love to this man who saw himself in me.

A quiet reserve fell over him; his movements stopped, and his eyes were still and unblinking. A half-peeled ginger in his hands dropped into the sink, and his lips cracked open but didn't form words, even though I was sure he'd heard the question.

I waited for him to stumble out a yes, but I know now that change will never come. I didn't ask again.

OUTSIDE, IN THE graying evening, as we walked to the bodega by the street corner, a boy who looked no older than twelve walked up to us. It was really JV he walked up to.

"My man," JV called out. His accent and persona were different.

Their handshake was swift, peppered with finger snapping.

"Hey, Uncle, can I try you today?" the boy asked JV.

Before I could comprehend their conversation, they started.

In the air, one palm strikes the other: left palm to right palm.

Pause, then jerk hands to their sides before wobbling, and palms strike again. The handclapping game involved sudden pauses, surprising slaps, all laced with mischief about who could outwit the other. As they went on, I watched a small cluster of men in front of a row house, no more than twenty feet from the sidewalk where we stood. They were hunched over as they rolled a die and waited for it to end its uncertainty.

Hands to his side with no jerking or wobbling, JV burst out laughing. The game was done. The boy must have lost, because he said, "I will get you tomorrow, Big JV. Tomorrow!"

JV chuckled as the boy walked up a small flight of stairs and into the house he'd come out from. It seemed to me that a quick rain had passed.

Enyeribe Ibegwam was brought up in Lagos, Nigeria. A recipient of a Kimbilio Fellowship and a finalist for the Commonwealth Short Story Prize, his stories have appeared in *Auburn Avenue* and *Welter*. He has received grants from the Vermont Studio Center and the Elizabeth George Foundation. He lives near Lake Murray in Columbia, South Carolina.

EDITOR'S NOTE

"Tornado Season" by Marilyn Manolakas demonstrates characteristics that I look for in stories that *Alaska Quarterly Review* publishes: freshness, honesty, and a compelling subject. The story is set in 1954 in Oklahoma. It presents a fourteen-year-old protagonist, Harmon, who is preparing to leave home to get married. Her mother has died and the relationship with her father is fraught. The idiosyncratic voice that Manolakas creates is strong. Her vivid cast of characters is engaging. Emotionally and intellectually complex, this poignant coming-of-age story resonates in one's memory.

Ronald Spatz, Editor
Alaska Quarterly Review

TORNADO SEASON

Marilyn Manolakas

THE AIR IS creamy and astringent, electric on the tongue like sour milk. The wood is rotting on the old clapboard house, sweating off its paint in shaggy rafts of white. From a distance, it is the same color as the gray sky behind it, blistered with clouds. Harmon sits between rows of jumpy corn stalks with a bottle of Old Crow she found in the barn, watching the windmill's patient spin turn maddening. Her dad's old Ford half-ton comes clumsy up the dirt drive in front of her, and she thinks to herself, *I'm getting married next week, and I don't give a shitass who says what about it.* Harmon is fourteen.

She wants to borrow a dress and go to the Church of Christ one afternoon and have punch and bricks of store-bought ice cream afterward like everyone else who gets married in Dill City. She doesn't want to slink off to Texas. But in Texas, she doesn't need her dad to sign the papers, so that's what she'll do if she has to. She's heard that in the old days, girls her age could get married without permission in Oklahoma, but now it's 1954, and there are laws. Harmon has always wanted a real wedding, has been planning it since she was little and would mash her corn husk dolls against one another, so why does he want to take that away from her? She pitches the empty bottle into the stalks behind her and pretends to study the wide, flat tumult of the sky.

"Come on back to the house," her dad yells over his driver's-side window mottled with mimosa pods caught in bird shit. "I been out at the Bookouts'. We got to get in the cellar before it comes."

She stands up and whiskey-lurches toward him but then finds her gait, wishing there had been more than a few drinks left in the bottle. "I hate it in there. It's got all of Mama's jars and things. Besides, I don't want to be in the cellar with you."

"I don't know why you got to act so ugly." And then, a high hitch in his voice: "We got to go in there sometime, Harmon. I been saying we should clean up some of her things." And he's looking not at her but past her, past the blackening sky. She feels a thrum of ache opening up in her throat, and she knows it's the least she can do for him, to just get in the cab. The springs of the leather bench creak against her weight as she slides in next to him, and the truck goes bouncing along toward the new house on the other side of the farm.

He looks over the big steering wheel in his lap toward her feet and says, "Wish you'd stop running around barefooted, nothing but stickers and cow patties out here."

"I look where I'm going."

He inhales some air between his teeth and then pauses. "Harmon, I saw that bottle. You can't be acting this way. Where'd you even get that thing?"

"It was in the old barn."

"Uh-huh."

"It was. Why don't you trust me about anything?"

"Well, you're still not supposed to be drinking it, wherever you got it from."

In the close cab she can smell the tractor grease on him and his nasty old Swan soap. She can smell herself, too, her new rayon dress trapping the sharp spice under her arms in a way her old feed-sack dresses, the cotton calico ones her mama used to sew for her, never had.

Her lips are dry and furrowed, crepe paper glued together at the ends, and she struggles to rip them apart and find something pleasant to say. "You know, Jimmy says they don't have tornadoes in Dallas, not really."

"Is that right?" He doesn't take the bait. Jimmy is twenty and a mechanic in the Air Force. He used to be stationed in the next town over, in Burns Flat, but then he transferred back to Carswell in Dallas. He's supposed to come get her sometime this week, just as soon as he gets a place for them to rent sorted out. He told her this on the phone six days ago, the heavy receiver hot on her cheek, her dad's eyes pressing in on her from the divan. He hasn't called since.

"Don't you want me to get away from the tornadoes?"

"You got to help me get the chickens in the chicken house so they don't blow away."

"Fine." She looks out at the crazed landscape stewing, dislodged thistles hopping along, insane, getting caught in the barbed-wire fence under the gathering ink of sky. She hopes Jimmy comes back soon. She misses him living near her, misses his neat blond body and the fug of his gritty sheets at night. She misses the wallop of something animal when she runs up to hug him, his musky cologne mixed with a powerful jolt. She'd sneak out of her house and meet his truck down the gravel road, and they'd spend a few hours in his little rented room. It's all she can hardly think about—his hands on her hips, his long eyes and long feet, and the bright, white-hearted thrill of losing the borders of herself in the dark at night. Her first time with Jimmy had hurt, and what she had enjoyed most in those first weeks was just the way he looked at her, like she was one of the necessities of life. After a while, though, she started to look forward

to it. Their hours together turned the rest of the world into a waiting room, everything else wrung-out and gray by comparison. Can
her dad tell that this is all she thinks about? Can everybody?

They get out of the truck in front of the brick house her mama
barely got a chance to fuss over, and the wind picks up, cracking at
the skeletons of fence-row trees, pockmarks of dry earth displaced
by scattered drops of rain.

"Here it starts," her dad says, and they begin to run at the chickens, a flurry of jittery white that they shoo in the low door. Scrabbly
lightning veins across the sky trailed by hard, flat thuds of thunder.
"We got to get some candles from the house so we don't break our
necks down there," he says, the rain now addressing her skin in
sharp, needling jabs.

They scurry through the back door of the house into the new
kitchen, dishes piled up on the yellow Formica, the shut-up smells
of dust and fresh paint and old dinners. Not that they eat much
anyway, lately. Harmon usually fixes some eggs, maybe some bread
or a glass of milk, maybe some green beans for dinner, but that's it.
Everything they eat, by the time they eat it, is perched on the edge
of rot. And neither of them clean up anything. Sometimes Little
Mama comes over, the old lady's chin bristling with dark glossy
hairs, white strings of spit webbing across the sides of her mouth
as she talks, and she says, "Harmon, someone has got to do something about this place. I didn't raise your mama not to teach you
how to keep up a house," but then she leaves, and Harmon does
nothing. Her dad doesn't mind.

Flicking the light switch back and forth, he says, "Nothing doing. Where did Pauline keep the candles?"

"How should I know? I won't be needing them in Dallas."

"Go look while I fill up some jugs."

She stands in the pantry, but she can barely see, the sun suffocated by the black clouds outside the kitchen window and everything getting darker by the second. So many extra cans of food that she used to play with, stacking up pyramids and fortresses and castles. Sometimes there'd be a dented one, and it wouldn't stack right, and she'd ask her dad if she could throw it away, and he'd just laugh at her. He had been forced to leave home as a teenager, back when nobody had any food and the evil dirt was blowing and his family was living in a chicken coop. He left Oklahoma to go pick onions in California, a time he doesn't talk about except to say that no one is allowed to bring any onions into the house, ever. Her mama was a good cook, and just about every recipe calls for onions, but she always minded him anyway.

Harmon looks under the sink, next to the soap and a sagging box of Brillo pads, and then she looks in the hutch with her mama's good Desert Rose plates, and there she finds them, in the cabinet next to their brass holders with the finger loops. She grabs the candles and stacks them in a paper bag from the TG&Y along with some of the candle holders and the old army lighter, and then she slides her thumbs through two of the holders and walks around spinning them, waiting for her dad to finish filling the jugs, grenade strobe of lightning flashing the room bright and dark.

The water cuts off while her dad is filling a big O'Halloran's Dairy jug from the tap. "Goddammit!" he says, and suddenly she's so sick of being in this kitchen with him, so sick of everything. A sibilance of wind finds its way through the insulation, juniper branches scraping at the windows, and she hears a treble of shattered glass, probably the wind kicking some loose object against the house—it's happened before.

But then there is the unmistakable low murmur of a human

voice pitched against the clang and roar of the thunderstorm. It sounds like someone is upstairs, cursing.

She holds her breath, pinned in place, the whiskey jagged in her empty stomach. Her dad stops fussing with the caps on the jugs and stands up straight as a telephone pole. One of the candle holders slips off her thumb.

"Hush! Be still." His eyes are wide and mean. The upstairs voice has gone quiet. "I'm going to go see. You stay down here."

"You don't get to boss me anymore!"

"Shh! Stop your hollering!"

She quiets down to a whisper-bite and says, "What if something happens? Little Mama said she saw the devil up there!"

After a moment, he gives a horsey exhalation in her direction and starts up the stairs, but then he comes back and picks up a squat pewter lamp from the hutch, thwapping it against his other hand to test its weight. She follows him up the stairs, and in the dark of the stairwell, his gibbous face angles toward her, but he doesn't try to stop her. When he reaches the shadows of the balustrade at the landing, he pauses and then opens up her bedroom door, asking her, "Anything look different?" and she shakes her head, happy to be useful. They march on to the extra bedroom, the same quilts and Grandma Matilda's Shaker furniture as usual, and she feels a deflating prick of disappointment at the vanishing drama of her life. They cross into her parents' room, and no excitement there either, until she notices one of her mama's pretty things—the Limoges box, she thinks—nestled in the carpet in shards. The door to the adjoining bathroom is open, so she turns toward it, and there they are.

There are two of them, boys she recognizes from the town across the highway, caught in the silvery light. The big one is named Cecil, but she doesn't know the little one's name. She doesn't go to school with them, but she's seen them at the drugstore and at football games and Sunday school parties. Her dad grabs at the soggy back of her dress, lift of cool air sent up her spine, and steps in front of her. Something long is in Cecil's hand, and now he's raising it, pointing it at her dad. He puts up his hands, useless lamp hoisted in the air, and backs into the bedroom a few paces. After a moment, the boys follow.

"Don't point that at him, stupid," the little one says, jump of fear in his voice.

"How do you know he's not going to tell?"

"So you're going to shoot him, shithead?" Only now, staring at her grandpa's old Winchester '94, does the warm whiskey leave her all at once, replaced by a mealy headache and a sour clench at her throat.

Her dad lowers his hands, sets the lamp on the bedside table, and speaks to them in a deep, even register: "You boys should know that thing ain't even loaded. Weren't you going to check?"

"We was just borrowing it to go shoot some turkeys," Cecil says.

"Okay. Well, fair enough. But you won't get many turkeys without any bullets. So how about you give it back right now, and I won't call Clifton Black as soon as the lights come back on?"

"Huh-uh." Cecil is tall with a stout, proud stomach showing through his overalls like a man's, but he's still young in the face, a boy hesitating to blow out his birthday candles so all eyes stay fixed on him.

"Let's just give it to him," the little one says.

"We ain't giving back shit! We just come out all this way." But after a thick moment, he lowers the gun shakily. Harmon takes an easy breath, adrenaline leaving her body in waves. She is very tired.

"Aren't you Glenn Fight's boy?" her dad asks the little one.

"Yessir."

"Dumbass! Who's stupid now?"

"She knows who we are anyway," the little one says, pointing at Harmon, and it's true, more or less. They're her age. She's always known them as shy, obedient boys, nodding politely at adults and sitting off to the side at church mixers. There's never any telling about people.

"What's your name, son?" Her dad's eyes never leave the black shape of the rifle, still hanging from Cecil's left hand with the front sight touching the floor.

"Verle, sir."

"Okay, Mr. Verle Fight. Well. A tornado might be coming for us soon. Why don't you tell your friend to give me back my dad's rifle, and we can all get down in the cellar? If there's any turkeys left, you can shoot them after." In the dresser mirror, she can see her dad wink at Verle. She's never seen him wink before.

Verle regards her dad blankly for a second and then looks at Cecil and says, "I don't want that old thing anyhow. I thought they'd have better stuff." Harmon feels a scorching touch of shame at the thought that they didn't have anything nicer to steal.

Cecil asks Verle, "What about my brother's car?"

"We left our car by the highway," Verle says to her dad.

"Don't worry about that. Big tornado'll smash a car whether it's on the highway or not. Hey, now, how about I got ten dollars in my billfold, and I'll buy that old thing back from you?"

Cecil considers this and then hands over the gun tentatively. Her dad takes hold of it by its cracking walnut stock and points it toward the ground. She thinks she hears an iced-over edge come into his voice as he says, "All right, then. Cellar's in the yard. You boys go first. You can have your ten dollars after this thing passes."

Her dad makes her walk behind him as they all shuffle outside, sheets of rain reigniting the scent of her VO5 Creme Rinse. "It's raining bullfrogs!" he says to her, trying to lighten the mood, she can tell. As she watches his rangy figure tread in front of her, his tired, flat-footed splay, she feels a twinge of guilt for the way she's been talking to him. He's so good, and he works so hard, and he's being so good with these stupid, stupid boys. And he's so nice to her, despite everything, despite the fact that if it weren't for her, her mama would still be here. She should behave herself. But then, he's trying to take away her one chance to have a wedding, isn't he?

He stoops over and grunts as he opens the door in the cement driveway by the side of the house. Harmon drops down into the lightless night of the cellar, assailed by dank air and an ungodly stench that she doesn't recognize. They file in behind her, and she flicks the lighter, looking around among the milk crates and canning jars and bric-a-brac for the source of the smell, and she thinks she sees something, an old mouse on its back marked with white gashes of decay.

"Harmon, give me that."

Her dad takes the lighter, the flame doubling when the wick catches on the first candle, and then he melts the end of it and sticks it in its brass circle. The boys sit on the floor in a corner, so she sits in the corner opposite them, as far away as the tight space permits, wedged between two boxes and an old steamer trunk.

She looks over at the boys and considers them, the flame lapping at their greasy faces, making them look febrile, crazed. She thinks about Cecil, about his bulbous mouth and two slippery eels for eyes. If she didn't marry Jimmy, would she have to make do with a scrap of affection for a boy like that? She didn't want to chance it.

"We thought you'd be down here already," Verle offers, as if this were a pleasant impromptu social call. Verle has dark grass stains on the knees of his denims and a haircut that looks like someone gave it to him in a hurry.

"Is that right?" her dad says, tending to the rest of the candles on the floor, sitting on his haunches in the center of the low room, the long rifle parked by his side.

As he works, the shaky candle-jump light catches the tattoos that peek out beneath the rolled-up sleeve of his shirt. Harmon has never known what to make of them. They split open her understanding of him, leave her with the same queasy feeling she got the time she accidentally walked in on her parents making love one Sunday afternoon. Almost like that, but not quite. Every time someone mentions his tattoos, the scumbled eagle and dagger on his upper arm, relics from his time in California, he stammers a few words about being young and then changes the subject. Her dad, such a dependable member of the Church of Christ, so shy in crowds that nobody even makes him read the scripture out loud like all the other grown men—the fact of these tattoos is inexplicable to her. Sometimes she catches glimpses of something—some youth, some violence in his eyes—that makes her think she understands, but then she loses it. Like when he clubs rabbits in the garden with an old wagon spoke and seems immune to their wheezing screams. Or when he laughs with his old friend Otto and they talk about how they used to have to take baths in the creek with one bar of soap to share between them. But mostly those tattoos remain improbable, alien on the skin of the man she knows as her father.

She leans against the cold wall behind her, the wet fabric of her dress revealing the slope of her legs underneath, and she tries to sink back into herself, into a series of forced daydreams about Jimmy: his wide shoulders, the black outlines of his mechanic's fingernails, his mouth on the transparent skin of her breasts. The first time he asked her to be on top, she was embarrassed at first, but then something else happened, a connection made between being with him and the way she would rub herself against her bed at night. She started concentrating, gathering the threads of it, and then there it was—dizzying, boundless, like air or water or light. The first time he saw her shudder and pulse, he was surprised, shooting her an embarrassed grin after they were done. "Where'd you learn to do that?"

"By myself, I guess."

"Well, shit." And he started tickling her, she thought, to end the moment.

There was such a difference, wasn't there, between before and after? Before, she was so necessary. Sometimes, they wouldn't even get as far as the fields along the highway, and they'd pull over and he'd put his hand up her skirt, and even when it wasn't pleasure, it was the pleasure of being so urgently useful. They'd get to his room, and they'd take off their clothes and go weightless, and she would think: This is it. This is all she wants. How could anyone want anything else? The hot ferment of his breath on her neck: *You're my girl. My girl. Mygirlmygirlmygirl.*

And then: separation. Shy and embodied. Bashful drop of his eyes, put-on smile, plunging back to the ordinary objects of this room that smells like feet. Flea jump of anxiety at her throat: He always wants to get up and forget about her, make a cup of coffee on his hot plate or turn on his new TV. After is a demotion. She is at best decent company. She has so little to offer him. One time, she offered to sew a button back on one of his shirts, and he said no, in the Air Force they taught you how to do that yourself. A boy her age would have obliged, even if he knew how. After, she feels bereft, thick sheen of his come down her thighs in the bathroom glare, her pubic hair slicked wet and mossy. She stares at herself in the mirror, at the rinds of moon shadow beneath her eyes, and she thinks about how she should eat more but never does. She knows that, even though she's too skinny, she still looks like her mama, that she has her big dark eyes and round mouth, and she knows that this is why there will always be another time.

The last night she saw Jimmy before he left for Dallas, he seemed—more than usual, even—as though he was in a hurry to drive her home, and she sat in his truck looking out the window at the flat wash of the blue horizon, slip of moon peeking through the clouds. That Davis Sisters song was playing on the radio, "I Forgot More Than You'll Ever Know," and she wondered if this was something she could say to another girl about Jimmy and mean it. She wondered if he saw other girls. Her new house sat at the end of the driveway, so tight-lipped and dim, like nothing she even recognized, a broken-off bit of nothing much against the tumbling vastness of the storm-lamp sky.

The sounds of the rain are doubling, tripling over themselves against the cellar door. The wind bangs it ajar and then closed again, over and over. Her dad comes and sits next to her on the steamer trunk, the .30-30 perched in his lap.

She tries to think about something good, something pure. Images of her mama bead across her thoughts, but the one that gets caught in her mind is an image of her naked, the splayed breasts and dark pubic hair that Harmon glimpsed the night they had to get dressed for bed in the extra room at Little Mama's house. Why is this the mental picture of her mama that comes to her most often? She has been infected with sex. She needs to get out of here. Out of this cellar, this house, this town. She stares at the blank-faced darkness of the wall behind her dad. There is nothing she can do for him anymore.

So her dad didn't like Jimmy, fine, but that doesn't mean he has to take away her happiness. She can't imagine going the rest of her life without ever having a wedding. And she doesn't know what she'd do if she didn't have Jimmy to think about. She already has a hard enough time avoiding the high, keening ache for her mama.

Most of the girls she knew had mothers who were tough, brittle, strict. At their houses, she'd sit stiff as a bolt of fabric and try to seem sweet and godly. At home, she was allowed to think her thoughts and do as she pleased. To check out how-to-draw books from the library and spend afternoons copying down the ships and fashion plates. To read in bed all day and eat candy until dark. Sometimes she'd read a novel, like *The Caine Mutiny*, and love it so much that she'd get all excited and tell the entire book to her mama, chapter by chapter, and her mama would listen, really listen, and then tell her that she loved seeing the way her eyes lit up when she was talking about her stories. They'd sit up late together playing cards and drinking hot Dr Pepper with melted Red Hots at the bottom. When Harmon got in trouble at school, her mama would shrug and tell her dad that she was probably just smarter than all the other kids and bored. "Your mama let you have your way too much," her dad said once recently, but she didn't see it that way. Harmon had been born with a twin—a boy—who had died as a baby and had to be buried in a number-11 shoebox in a grown man's coffin since that was all they had left at the funeral home. Harmon always figured this made her mama more grateful.

And now the sounds of the rain are pinging against the cellar door, and it's choking her, this guilt, and she tries not to look at the dark shapes of the blackberry preserves her mama set up right before she died. She tries to focus her thoughts on Jimmy, but then Verle interrupts her.

"I reckon we could play a game?"

And Harmon hates him, she really hates him. His pitiful hair. Why is he in her cellar? "No one wants to play a game with you, shit-for-brains!"

Over Cecil's braying laugh, her dad says, "Harmon. Where'd you learn to talk like that?"

"Why would we want to play a dumbass game with someone who tries to rob us?"

She feels the hold of his eyes on her, watches the buckle of his mouth as he considers scolding her. "I have a game. It's called questions. I ask questions, and you all answer them."

She doesn't know if her dad is serious.

"First question: What do you boys think a twenty-year-old wants with marrying Harmon? You think I should just let her go get married?"

The boys hold themselves very still, looking down, and she is so ashamed. But after a moment, she sees Verle look up and absent himself from his face as he considers an answer. "Could be that he's lonely, sir. Not a lot of women his age around here. A lot of people moving to the city."

The city. These girls who graduate and move to Oklahoma City. She'd have to wait so long if she didn't marry Jimmy.

"Could be. Maybe Mr. Verle Fight's brains ain't so bad after all. Then again, I don't know. I don't know about this one." One of the candlewicks crackles, shoots a spark twirling to the floor. "Next question: What was you boys doing in my house?"

"We just wanted to shoot some turkeys, we told you!" Cecil says, voice nasal and sullen.

"Come on now."

Verle sighs a long sigh, and Harmon hates him even more, like he has any reason to be sad, coming over here and taking their things. "We was looking for some jewelry. Then we broke that little jewelry box with nothing in it and saw the gun hanging on the wall."

"What were you going to do with jewelry? You got a lot of girl-friends or something?"

"We were going to sell it. In the city. I want to start learning to rodeo. The junior division? Takes money, and my dad's been sick."

"I was pulling your leg, Mr. Verle. I knew you didn't have any girlfriends. And you broke one of my wife's good things. Next question: Harmon, what do you think it's like in Dallas? Do you think it's a good place to live?"

This question troubles her. She's worried about the water in Dallas. She can't even stand to drink the water in town. It's so sweet and soft, filmy on the tongue. She likes their hard cistern water on the farm, water that slakes your thirst with a bite of something me-tallic on the end. And Jimmy said his mother likes to wear hats and that he was going to buy Harmon a new hat from Foley's to wear when he introduces her to his parents. Wearing hats isn't really the thing around Dill City, not except for at church.

"I think it's probably better there. People are smarter."

"Do you think God wants this for you?"

Does he? Is her mama with God now? Church of Christ women have to sit mutely while the men do everything. Do they sit mutely in heaven too? Other kinds of people, like the Baptists, let their women sing and read. They even have instruments. Maybe it was more like that. But then again the Baptists said that the Church of Christ didn't baptize right—a prim little sprinkle instead of a dunk—and that if you don't get baptized right, you go to hell, so maybe it was better to hope they were wrong. Mostly, it seems like God goes about his own business and she goes about hers. Before her mom died, the Holy Spirit did seem alive in the church some Sundays though, in the preacher's thunderous voice, the great, roundhousing energy that echoed through the room, the curlicued spirals of logic that clenched a final place in her heart—*We know God loves us because the Word lives*—but then she'd go home and everything would be the same. As far as she was concerned, God could work his side of the street and she'd work hers. Lately she sits in church and thinks only about Jimmy.

"What I think is that God loves other people more than me."

"Harmon Lee, don't talk like that."

Harmon Lee. Her dad says it, like a lot of people's dads say their middle names, when he's mad, but her mom would always say it when she was happy. *Harmon Lee Sweetheart. Harmon Lee Sweetheart.* Oh Jesus she has to get out of this cellar.

"I have a question," Verle says. He had been watching this conversation, rapt, absorbing its moments with little exhalations and faces. He needed to mind his own damn business. "Where's your wife?"

"How stupid are you? Why are you asking questions? My dad asks the questions."

"She passed," her dad offers.

"Oh." Verle looks panicked, searching the air above him for something to say. "I'm sorry. How, how'd she die?"

"Don't you know that's not polite, dumbass?"

"It's all right. She was in an accident. Painless. It happened real suddenly. She's in heaven now."

Nobody seems to know what to say, so nobody says a word. How is her dad so sure that her mama's in heaven? And, *suddenly*, that word. Like all the words people have used about her mama since she died, especially at the funeral, there's something sideways about it. Harmon has relived that day so many times. She's sick of hearing this singsong version of it offered up to people who don't even matter.

It was almost suppertime. Cotton-chopping season. The sun dipped low and the heat hung back. Her mama in the doorway of her room. *I'm all cooped up in here. Let's go for a drive and get us a Dr Pepper from town.* Harmon putting down her old copy of *Little Women* and getting up from her prone position on the bed, unwholesome ache in her belly from eating Sugar Babies all day in the dark. *I keep telling you that's bad for your eyes.* Hot wind on the sweaty hair stuck to her forehead. *You drive, Harmon, I'm tuckered out.* Why? Why did she agree to drive? What if her brother had lived, and he had driven instead? What if her brother had lived and she hadn't?

To say something happens suddenly is to forget that everything happens suddenly. But there are some moments that heave more weight onto themselves than our minds can bear. The Plymouth turning out from the bowling alley, striking them headlong and lifting. The truck sent spinning. Sheeting shrapnel of glass, light in the air, hanging, pealing down on her in cuts, cuts, cuts. Her mama pitched through the windshield, floating, up and up, and then the truck's heavy whirl, around and around and into the ditch, Harmon's head against the metal door.

And then the icy surface of something, fleet on the face of it, skating light, falling through, plunging. The man pulling on her. Putting her on a stretcher like a lank doll. *Where is she? Where is she? I need to put my head on her jelly chest and cry about this. Goddammit, I need her.*

Oh, her mama. She was beautiful, that wrecked word. It doesn't

even touch what all she was. The photo of her in her dad's wallet
that drew him back from California, back to this town, this farm
that had once belonged to her parents. Doe-eyed, dark-lipped, the
rest of her life shining forth from her eyes looking up and to the
right of the camera.

Into this spiraling silence, her dad's voice breaks like a clay pigeon, shattering across the air. "Harmon, I can't let you get married in the church. It's a sin, being with him. I don't think any of
this is right." He pauses for a second. Opens his mouth, then closes
it. Then he says, "I heard you leave at night, Harmon."

And the rain has slowed down to hard, staccato bursts, and
this is the worst kind of shame, that he said this in front of these
ridiculous boys.

"Do you think he'll be good to you?"

"No. I don't really think so." And as soon as she says it, she
knows it's true, is visited by it, this radiating knowledge that doesn't
change a single thing about her plans to marry him.

She met Jimmy at the drugstore in Cordell two months after the
funeral. She'd take the Buick after school while her dad was still
out with the workers, and she'd sit there at the counter, drinking
dun-colored coffee heaped with high piles of sugar and cream. She
liked reading the women's magazines, the articles about skincare
regimens and ideas for ways to busy herself creating colorful finger
foods for her husband when he got home from work. They made
life seem conquerable. She hated being at home. Sometimes Karen
and Carolyn would come sit with her, and they'd talk about the
boys, but most days they had chores.

The first time Jimmy spoke to her, he sat down next to her and
said, "You look like a girl who wants to go to the rodeo with me
next weekend."

She was startled at first, but then she considered his uniform, his cheekbones, his slick smile. She decided she was probably lucky.

"I love the rodeo."

He put his hand on hers for one jolting moment and asked, "What's your name?"

She told him, and he said, "Harmon. That's different."

"It was my grandpa's name. And then it was my brother's name. But he died, so they gave it to me."

He studied her face. "How old are you, anyway?"

"Fourteen."

"I would have guessed sixteen at least." And it was true, she did look older lately, with her face painted up to match the saturated colors of her store-bought clothes. Carolyn had pierced her ears just the week before with an ice pick and an old piece of potato. That fall, instead of winding her wet hair around curlers every night, the way her mama used to do for her, she started getting her hair set once a week at the beauty shop, unsticking it from her scalp in the morning with a pick reeking of Spray Net. She had also stopped wearing her glasses on account of the fact that her homework had always been too easy for her anyway. She looked like her mama now—everyone said so.

"Does that mean you don't want to take me anymore?"

"You don't have to be sixteen to go to the rodeo."

From that point on, all that mattered was Jimmy.

The cellar is getting colder. She can't sit still, can hardly stand herself, shivering and smelly, her dad's watchful gaze filling up the room, headache growing more insistent. She gets up to move her body, to look around at all of this detritus the two of them have been avoiding so assiduously. Boxes of quilts bubbled with holes that expose the batting, stiff nursing uniforms that smell like dust and rot, an old black iron that once belonged to her Choctaw great-grandmother. Her mama's high school recipe cards, and the coursing energy of her looping scrawl, returned from the dead right there in blue ink. A sack of something lumpy and fetid behind the boxes. Harmon reaches for it, holding her nose as she picks it up, and then dangles it away from her. Onions. A sack of onions. And she can feel a grin spread across her face. What would her mama want with a sack of onions, anyway? She didn't cook with them.

"Lookit, Daddy. Mama's got onions down here."

She holds them up, the stench stinging her nostrils, and he looks pained for a moment, but then he laughs and then laughs again, and he keeps going, far more laughter than she's comfortable with in her dad, really, these laughs that don't even work right—he hardly makes any noise and just bats at the air with his hands a little as his face turns red. It's embarrassing.

Cecil looks over at her dad, elbows Verle, and says, "Don't take much to get him going, does it? He better quit or he'll piss hisself," and then Cecil starts laughing too, showily, Harmon thinks, peacocking for Verle.

Finally, her dad says, "I just *knew* that's what it was. Well, Pauline. I swear. Thank you for that. I needed it."

Harmon sits back down, a lopsided smile finding its way to the disused muscles of her face, and the rain slows to an intermittent tap on the cellar door, and then it stops. Her dad picks up the rifle and blows out the candles, one at a time, smoke tailspinning.

"Well, let's get, I guess."

He opens the hatch to the outside, abrupt light closing the aperture of her eyes in a spasm. They climb up the ladder and stand in the driveway, shot through with sunset all at once. The sky is enormous, alien, belonging to some other kind of planet, pressing down on them in pinks and blues and purples. In the mixed-up landscape of the yard, tree branches, two-by-fours, lawn chairs are stranded wildly, shipwrecked. The air is now sweet and flat and settled. "Guess it missed us," her dad says. Their overgrown garden sits neglected by the patio, and the silhouettes of something fidgety—rabbits—are shaking the ragged foxtail between the heads of cabbage pocked with dark marks of rot.

"The rabbits came out," Harmon says, pointing toward them. Her dad looks her in the eyes for a vacant moment, and then, in one floating motion, he lifts the rifle and presses its wooden stock to his cheek, clicks back the hammer, and sends an echoing shot toward the garden. The rabbits scatter.

Her dad turns toward the boys, who look startled, unsure about what happens next. "You boys better get home before I call Clifton Black."

As she watches their hunched shapes recede toward the road, she hears the far-off hum of an engine growing louder. A new truck is gliding up the road toward the house, crunching the gravel, the thin, twining vocals of a country song blaring distantly. The truck is red and white, flat-nosed, sharp—it's Jimmy's new truck, and she jumps to smooth the static of her hair, to wipe the mascara under her eyes onto her thumbs. Her bare feet are caked in dirt, and she hadn't noticed until now that she's bleeding from her toe a little, a notch missing from the hard skin above her big toenail. She looks at her dad, picking up the lumber from the yard and putting it back in its pile on the back porch. Her stomach turns over. A hollow, swallowing place opens up in her. What's he going to do here by himself? She'll have to come back and visit all the time, then. Dallas is only five hours on the highway, four if you drive real fast. She'll be back.

Jimmy parks in front of her, gets out of the cab, and reaches his hands in the air. "Whew! I did not think I was going to make it. I've been trying to call you all week! It just rings and rings."

And she looks at him, standing underneath the lurid wall of collapsing sky. He doesn't look quite the way she remembers. The expression on his face is not one she knows.

Marilyn Manolakas lives in Iowa City. Her short fiction has appeared or is forthcoming in *New England Review*, *Alaska Quarterly Review*, and *Santa Monica Review*. She is at work on a novel about 1970s Los Angeles.

EDITOR'S NOTE

When I first read "Cicadas and the Dead Chairman" by Pingmei Lan, I was moved by its quiet oddity and its rendering of an unusual relationship between the child narrator and a woman she knows as the old maid. The world drawn is cruel, but there are transcendental pockets in the relationships between renegades. Lan captures how women who subvert their prescribed roles become in local rumor creaturely, mythological. They become mysterious life forms illegible to the disciplinary gaze of the conventional. They are often despised. Yet Lan's narrator describes the old maid devotionally, and their friendship is a brief silo where they can run strange together. In the end, this is a tragic narrative, one that clasps shut around the old maid's disappearance from the narrator's life, or from life entirely. I read it and was stunned by the wake it left.

Tracy O'Neill, Editor in Chief, 2018
Epiphany

CICADAS AND THE DEAD CHAIRMAN

Pingmei Lan

THAT SUMMER WHEN Chairman Mao died I saw a funeral for the first time, a national one. It had gone on for weeks. Everywhere I turned, people were wearing black armbands and making white paper flowers. The usual sea of blue Mao suits seemed to be foaming, churning, shaping into dark and light swells. Thousands of mourning wreaths blanketed Tiananmen Square, eventually spilling down to the sidewalks of Chang'an Avenue. For days, then weeks, it looked like snow in summer.

Then an old farmer came to Beijing riding a donkey cart. He cried over Mao's body while waving his copy of the Little Red Book. The Chairman looked down at this loyal subject from an old photo hung above the Tiananmen Fort. A half smile flashed permanently between his smooth pink cheeks and bright black beauty mark. The farmer made the news after crying for days and passing out, his fingers brittle and curled over the good book.

I didn't understand that kind of devotion and grief, having just turned seven that spring. And the only thing I knew about death was from the old maid who lived across the hutong.

"My lover died and came back to life," she said one day.

I walked away without answering. I didn't know if she was crazy. I didn't know if she was talking to me.

She was sitting on her doorstep, watching the clouds move and threading her fingers through her hair. Everyone in the hutong gossiped about how she had gotten that *creepy head of white hair* when she was only twenty-six.

She never ate salt. (Eat your salt or your hair would turn like that.)

She lived in a cave for ten years and ate mushrooms that grew on the walls.

She was a white snake who turned into this thing when she ate the magic ginseng roots from the Manchurian mountains.

I preferred to think of her as having been born that way, with hair frosted by Yan Wang's brew to prove her connection to the underworld. Her eyes too, they had this dark pull, at once mercurial and warm. Her lashes were pale and shiny like the hooks fringing a Venus flytrap. I imagined men who inched closer, willing to latch on. They'd follow her into this other place, where gremlins made decisions to either feast on the dead or send them back to life untouched. The old maid—no one knew her name, so we called her that—was the only one who could sway that decision one way or the other.

ONE DAY, I decided to ask Dad about the old maid. My parents were propaganda writers for the Department of Education eager to please their party secretary. Dad, however, had a bad cough from his days in an education camp. So sometimes he gazed out the window when he was supposed to be working. This is what he was doing while Mom slaved over "Virtues of China's Own Brand of Democracy."

When I approached Dad, Mom looked up from her desk. "Shut up," she said. "Have you done your calligraphy today?" She fished out a book of Mao's poetry, rice paper, and her calligraphy kits, and told me to copy ten poems.

The stench of her ink mill made me gag. But I held my breath and sat next to her. The ink stick bled, diminishing as I ground it against the stone water tray.

When mom left to go look up something at the National Library of Beijing, I went to Dad. He handed me a five-fen coin and whispered, "Go! Play outside and get a snack or something," but he did not speak of the old maid.

It WAS ONE of those thirty-nine-degrees-Celsius days. Sunlight bounced onto every surface, until even the dingy outhouse walls glared like sheet metal. The old maid was sitting on her steps, mumbling to herself, her skin pale for someone who sat in the sun so much.

We walked to Drum Street to get a slice of watermelon.

Near the fruit-and-vegetable stand, a group of men were unloading boxes of tomatoes. They stopped their work and watched us, their eyes darting up at the old maid. Her shirt was open, with several buttons missing. I hardly noticed it then, having seen her dressed like that year-round. But the men must have been new to the neighborhood. Their mouths fell open, and I could see their yellow teeth thrusting above swollen gums.

The tallest man shouted, "Hey, honey, come here!" He was staring at this heart-shaped mole between her breasts. It looked like a button that could open some kind of hidden door.

We tried to ignore him. The old maid covered her face with a sleeve while I picked a fat slice of melon from a neatly layered pile, despite the vendor's chiding.

The center of the melon was sweet and juicy. The old maid took the rest, the pink-white flesh along the rim. I'd always leave plenty for her. But more so on that day. I was uneasy with the men's hard eyes.

"Hey, want me to buy you a slice?" The man who had shouted earlier took a step forward and gave her a wink.

When she didn't answer, he took another step and lifted a hand as if to pet or to strike her. I couldn't tell. His knuckles were covered in scabs, either from working or from punching something hard, or both.

The old maid looked at me and I could see that she wanted to dash. That was one of the reasons I liked to hang around her. If I tried hard enough, I could read her thoughts.

We broke into a sprint, the last of the watermelon rind drawing a pink arc in the air. I must have muttered a curse as she shouted over me, "Shish . . . I *like* the rind!"

We ran down a block, then another, deeper into the maze of hutongs. After a few minutes, the only thing I could hear was the sound of our feet slapping the pavement. The men seemed to have given up. So we began to double back. As we ran, I could see the wind splitting her hair into light strands. They looked silvery, as if dissolving into streaks of moonlight.

"I can't breathe!" I crashed under the nearest pagoda tree.

The cicadas screamed. It made the hutong feel empty, vast.

"Shut up, shut up." The old maid plopped down next to me and shouted at the restless insects.

When I squinted, I saw a ball of white light bursting through the pagoda's canopy. Tian Gong, the sky's emperor, seemed to be staring down at it, or at me, with disapproving looks. When my eyes began to water, I turned to see the old maid lying down on her side. On the back of her neck was a blue-black bruise. I rubbed my eyes.

I was about to ask her about it when something small and hard fell on my head. I froze, a scream rasping in my throat.

She leaped up. "A cicada!" she said, picking the nugget of black out of my hair. "It's dead. That's why it was screaming. Her last song."

I breathed hard, unsure of what to say. She plopped back down to show me the cicada, then shoved it in her mouth. Maybe she only took a bite. Either way, a squirt of green liquid flew out, thin and curling, like a snake.

I shut my eyes. But it was too late.

She laughed and smeared something damp on my hand. "Look. Green blood. Isn't that cool? No red. No red. No red at all! That's what I like."

When I tried to reply that that was a dangerous thing to say, I threw up green bile.

She hopped up and stared blankly, as if I were morphing into a cicada with my eyes bulging, my skin cold and shiny, and a pair of bright sticky wings rubbing out desperate, screechy songs against my back.

As I said, the neighborhood had plenty to say about the old maid. The popsicle lady, for example, rolled up with her little wooden cart when she saw me with her and pulled me away.

"Don't you know that old maid is messed up in her head, crazy as a winter snake?" She patted my hair with her knobby, spotted hands. "They need to send her to an asylum. And comb her hair and find her a shirt that still has a button."

Opium Andy appeared out of nowhere to cut her off, his wife-beater riddled with holes that weren't supposed to be there. "No shit," he said. "But the retard isn't hurting anyone. Besides, in the West—that's the other side of the world—women walk around bare-chested. And men wear high-collared buttoned shirts. So it is *us* that got everything backwards."

I knew nothing about this other side, this Western world. It sounded like the underworld to which the old maid belonged. The hutong hushed as if to consider Andy's perspective.

The popsicle lady shook her head and touched her high collar. It pushed against her skin and made these folds on her throat. We padded farther down the street, her bound feet pecking the hot asphalt. She waited until Andy was out of sight. "You'd never know that he was a big opium ghost. What a handsome devil! Shame he's got such a pretty wife but no kids after all these years." Andy's wife, Char, was our neighbor, and she would talk up a storm with Mom nearly every day. Dad called her the Chain-Smoking Gossip Mill Operator when Mom wasn't around, which made Andy chuckle, and I kind of liked that. The popsicle lady continued. "I bet he's spreading his seed around somewhere else. Char is holding up more than half the sky, if you ask me."

It was a Chairman Mao saying. *Women hold up half the sky.* I was tired of hearing it. Maybe Andy was, too, and figured he wouldn't have to hold anything if he *spread it around.* But I liked hearing words like *opium ghost.* Nobody else said things like that to a little kid.

That night the moon was the size of Mom's dinner plate. No clouds. I watched the old maid's window through mine, thinking she might wave good night to me. The street got quiet after a while and a man came up and knocked on her glass. Then the window opened and he climbed inside. So it was true. She had a lover, and he'd come back for her.

I didn't like the idea. What if, this time, he snatched her away to the underworld?

The man didn't come out for days. And neither did she. I tried to peer through her window whenever the hutong was empty. But nothing materialized.

When she reappeared, a week later, her hair was all tangled and big. Her eyes looked weepy, red around the rims. When she turned her face I saw the bruise again. I wanted to ask her if her lover had come back and taken her somewhere. And did he leave again or did he die this time. But she wasn't in the mood to talk. In fact, she seemed to be sinking under oceans of water. My only connection to her was this string of thought bubbles I couldn't read.

I pretended I'd noticed nothing and sat next to her. Mom had said once, after I lost a balloon, "Forget about it." So I told the old maid the same thing.

She nodded and folded herself into a tight little ball. A few minutes later she shifted her head closer. Or maybe I was leaning toward her. Our heads touched, and it felt nice, her hair cool and hot like the dying flame on a candle. I kept trying to read her thoughts, but nothing came through. Our heads knocked gently against each other while splashes of summer poured.

Later, we washed our feet in the river near Temple Street, where the air was cool and damp. Along the banks, green summer worms slicked shiny trails over willow leaves while dragonflies dashed among floaters, drawing bright red arcs like upside-down smiles. We made a shrine by piling up pebbles under the pagoda tree. I

wrote "Peace Under the Other World" on a piece of paper and se-
cured it near the top. We bowed a dozen times and murmured non-
sense as prayers to silence her lover's lingering spirit.

Over that summer, the old maid and I added a few more things
to the little shrine. A button. A bottle cap. A pressed, flattened
cigarette-pack wrapper. Each commemorating the departure of
someone she called "her lover."

It never occurred to me to ask her whether there was more
than one.

People had stopped walking around in black armbands by then.
All the wreaths had disappeared from Tiananmen Square, too. The
giant photo of Chairman Mao remained on top of the Tiananmen
Fort as always, the beauty mark above his lips a hard black like
cicada shells.

During those weeks Mom and Dad occasionally fought around
dinnertime. One night, Dad banged on the table until it tilted, spilling a bowl of cabbage soup. The way his lips trembled gave me a
chill. I ducked under the table to catch bubbles of grease so they
didn't make the floor slippery. The shouting continued. Apparently
Mom should have considered marrying herself to work instead.
And Dad was perfectly capable of taking care of himself.

I, for once, didn't have much to say.

When they finally stopped yelling, Mom was shaking so much
her chair went *ta, ta, ta*. I thought about touching her hand, but
she stood up and tripped on me. Dad started cursing again. Mom
stomped to the big window and shuffled things on her desk. The
house was like a balloon ready to burst. I had to sneak away.

Outside, a dozen boys in the neighborhood were chasing the old
maid until they were up against the outhouse. She was wearing a
shirt that almost covered her. Still, it was open in the front.

The boys yelled, *Retard! Stinky shoe!* And they pushed her into a corner and tore at her shirt. Mom had shown me picture books about how the Red Guards had done such things, during the fat Chairman Mao years. However, I hadn't seen it in person. The boys narrowed their eyes, and the muscles on their faces quivered. They spat on the old maid as if she were a slab of the sidewalk.

I flapped my arms and opened my mouth but my voice was lost. My feet weighed a thousand pounds. A part of me was glad they ignored me as if I were nothing but a vision, a ghost. Another part of me wanted to break the little circle of boys wrapped around her.

When the boys left, I crept closer. Her shirt had fallen to her waist. Her hair was damp with spit; her hair was stuck to her chest. But she smelled like the outside, not stinky. I scooted until I was close enough to touch her or to shout into her ears, *Play time, watermelon time, run away time!* It was sort of our song. But I never got up the nerve.

She must have sensed I was there, but she couldn't seem to recognize me. It would be my first inkling that something was indeed not right about her. And it wasn't because I couldn't rescue her. Her body was rigid, her eyes hollow, so that things of this world seemed to be falling through, getting lost in a void. I could see that she'd gone to that other place where I couldn't follow, from where I couldn't try to bring her back.

Still, I lifted a finger toward her, willing her to touch me back, waiting, as my legs fell asleep, waiting.

It was nearly dark, so I was drifting off a bit when she split my eardrums with a long howl. Like the cicada's death song and its awful green blood, it made me want to scream.

Popcorn Sam came into the hutong and sang about his fluffy sweet popcorns. Soon a growing crowd of kids surrounded him.

I couldn't resist running up to join them, reaching out my dirty hands for a share. When the old maid howled again, my hands had become too full and my legs too stiff to turn back.

MOM WAS TALKING to Char when I finally made it home.

"I thought she was still an old *maid*. You know, untouched," Mom said, her hands busy scrubbing a pot. "Where is she hiding these men? I don't buy it." She clucked her tongue.

"Why not? She's got those soul-sucking eyes men leave their wives for." Char tapped on her cigarette and puffed out a line of smoke that sliced into the sky.

Mom shook her head hard. "No. Not Andy. No way. Listen, the retard's pretty but useless. Can't tell the yins from the yangs on a good day. She's practically old now. Andy's too high-minded."

"Better be." Char coughed a bitter laugh. "Or I'd break both their legs! I don't care if she is a witch or a snake monster or the Skeleton Ghost!"

Mom reiterated that the old maid was not worthy of worry. Then she turned inside with a stack of dishes. I paused near the door, unsure whether to back away or move forward. Char was quiet a second, turning on me next. "Where did *you* come from?" she said. "Were you hiding this whole time?"

"No," I said, irritated. "Are you talking about the old maid? And what does that have to do with *Andy*?"

Her face changed from pink to ashen. She grounded the cigarette butts littered around her feet until they made hissing noises. She slapped me hard. "Look at you," she said, "starting school soon and still hanging around that slutty old shoe!"

I snapped, "Is she older than you? I bet she runs faster than you barefoot. Are you jealous?" By then, I'd forgotten that Mom was close.

"Shut up!" Mom's voice shook me. I turned to see she was trembling and staring me down. "Go wash up."

I started to tell her about the old maid and the boys and Popcorn Sam and how his machine had exploded and threw up soot. But she shoved me inside before I could say another word.

"Shut up," she said. "Shut up, oh, Pusa, shut up!"

The moon was cold that night. Dad was coughing an awful cough when Mom finally came in to wash his feet, make tea. I peered out the window by my bed. One of the street lamps was out, so the rest struggled, hissing in the dark. A small mob of moths flew around the halos of the surviving bulbs, making an occasional dull clink. The old maid's window was an even shade of black.

I sank into my bed and listened to Mom and Dad peck at each other with words I didn't understand. My head throbbed. I tugged and pulled on the rubber band clutching my hair to loosen it.

After a while, Mom appeared by the side of my bed. "Want a hand?"

I nodded and sat up. She hadn't done this for days; it felt like ages.

After she detangled my hair, she combed it from root to tip. I took a deep breath and leaned into her hands. Her warmth seeped into my scalp, making me sleepy.

"What's that?" She pointed to my window. The panes were coated in layers of dust and mud splatter from winter snow and summer thunderstorms. But I had cleaned a small circle in the center, so moonlight was pouring through it.

"My secret portal. Everyone in the world passes through it," I whispered, my eyes half-closed as she rubbed my scalp. When she pulled forward to look, she forgot to let go of my hair.

"Ouch!" My eyes snapped open.

Mom was staring out at the street below, and the old maid's window. Perhaps another lover had returned. I didn't know. But Mom's face was far away and then really close. She told me to lie down, shut my eyes. Her voice a whisper but firm, tangled into my sleep. I dreamed she hovered there all night, her shadows keeping the moon from frosting my eyes.

FOR THE REST of the summer, Mom locked me in the house.

The house grew darker earlier as summer receded into fall. On one evening, I dipped a hand in the calligraphy ink tray and stamped the pages of *Chairman Mao's Poems* with spiraling impressions of my fingers. Each was a twisted vortex. I was on the verge of finger painting the walls when Mom came home.

The next day, she put away the padlock. School was starting. I was told to march straight from home to school and back again with an assigned walking group.

THE CIRCUMSTANCES OF me running away that fall have faded over the years. But I know it started with a note my teacher wrote. She had sent me home with it out of the blue, a few weeks into the semester. On the way home, I snuck out of the walking group and hid behind the outhouse wall. When the other kids called, I told them to go ahead.

Under the pagoda tree, I unfolded the note. It said that I'd never turned in my homework and that I got zero points on my quizzes. If things didn't change, I might not graduate first grade.

I read it again. The teacher's signature stared like menacing eyes.

"What's that?" The old maid plopped down next to me. I was happy to see her, but the letter weighed in my hands.

"It's school," I said, giving her a half wave, the paper flinging and making a tearing sound in the air. I hoped she would tear it and toss it over the roof.

But she patted it flat and licked around its corners before settling down and reading the note, her head jerking back and forth. Her words sounded slow and a little blurry. "Is this for your dad?"

"The teacher said I should get his signature."

"Will he get mad?" she asked.

"Probably," I said.

"Parents are mean," she said slowly, petting the paper, as if it were a hand, my hand. And somehow I felt better.

We sat awhile. When the sun began to breathe down our necks, she snapped off willow branches and made whistles out of leaves. We tried to make a song. Hers sounded good but I got a headache from trying. When she laughed at the way I puckered my lips, I laughed too.

The old maid braided two willow branches together and it started to look like a wreath. "You want to come live at my house?"

I wanted to say yes. But then she had a look.

"No," she said, changing her mind. "My lover will kick you. Plus, my mom's here now. That witch is a pain." She picked at a scar on her lips. It looked like a blister. "She only makes me want to run again," she said. I hadn't known that about her. Maybe some of the rumors were true. I tried to picture her running away, living in that magic cave, eating those mushrooms. "You should run too," she said, "have an adventure!" She darted in circles around the tree. The paper fluttered in her hand like a dove trying to get free. I pictured myself as that bird, flying south, where it was always summer.

I'd read about ancient heroes running away from their lives in
the old books. But I'd never thought I knew anyone who'd done it.
"Maybe I could take a bus!" I said, excited. "Then I won't get too
tired from running." It would be my first bus ride, too, I neglected
to say.

"You're right!" She flapped over to me and pulled me to a run.
We turned from the hutong onto Peaceful Underworld Avenue.
From there, the number 24 bus stop was only a block away.

The bus was crowded. The old maid had to jam a shoulder
against my back to push me through the crowd. No room for me to
turn around and wave goodbye to her, but I figured she'd already
left. The crowd smelled like fatigue, and they didn't care who was
getting squished. After a few stops, I found an open seat. The window was cracked and it was still bright out. An army of bicycles
rang their bells; some of the riders put a hand on the side of the bus
while they waited. The crowd had thinned on and off the bus as
the sky changed its colors. Pink, purple, dark blue, gray. The Drum
Tower looked big and forbidden for a second, then orange and gold,
becoming a paper cutout in the end.

The bus trudged forward, pushing away thick bubbles of night
air. I looked down and realized the letter was back in my pocket. I
didn't feel like reading it again. Besides, the driver had turned off
the inside lights. I closed my eyes.

"What's your name, little girl?" The driver looked at me through
his rearview mirror.

"Shut up," I said.

He looked kind, with curved lines around his eyes, but scary
too. I remembered then that the teacher had said *shut up* was not
my real name. But I couldn't remember the name she said after
that. So I curled into a corner of my seat and hid my face behind my

hands. The driver didn't ask me anything else, but drove me to the main bus station at the end of his route.

There, an old lady smiled at me in the street. I told her all about the old maid and about where I lived with my parents. The lady nodded and wrote in a notepad the whole time. Then she took me home on her bicycle.

THE POPSICLE LADY told me later that they took the old maid to an asylum for good. But I didn't believe it at first. Was it because of me? The question churned in my head. In the days that followed, a man came and sealed her door with red strips of paper, as if her house was the site of something bad, a murder, or an anti-revolutionary coup. There were whispers. *It was bound to happen.*

Char told me, "She's probably dead now in one of those places, so," winking, "forget about it."

I ran. And I stopped looking through my little portal. Mud soon reclaimed it. One day, I noticed my circle had re-blended with the rest of the glass. Not even my own fingers could trace a faint outline around it.

DAD FOUND THE teacher's note in my pocket the night I returned. After that, he changed his schedule so he could watch me do my homework and occasionally help Mom with dinner.

One night, Dad told me Opium Andy and Char were getting divorced. And Char was moving back to Mongolia. My parents had stopped calling me *shut up* then. I would never learn to read Mom's thoughts the way I could read the old maid's, and Mom never talked to me the way she talked with Char. Still, when she came to comb my hair, I sat close, and ran my fingers through hers after she was done. She sat quietly while I brushed, and for those few minutes I felt a strange, animal sound rattling inside her, a cry she had stuffed down for so long it'd gotten lost, couldn't find its way out. I kept brushing, but she must have sensed a pause in me, which made her say, "You are all grown up. Old enough to brush your own hair from now on."

Then she was gone.

In a few years, the city would eradicate *harmful insects*, including the cicadas. The old neighborhood would look immaculate, like a street maiden being forced to put on a new dress, her hair combed and stuffed in a bun so she looked garish and pretty, different. No leaves, broken wings, or smears of green blood remained on freshly swept streets. The old pagoda trees had been uprooted, replaced with neat rows of willows, planted at equal distances, like soldiers marching in parades. The district around the hutong, in fact, was left in an eerie quiet, its last scream exorcised from a tidy, balled-up body. I strolled among the hutongs, alone, listening and waiting for a familiar pair of eyes to emerge, thoughts unread, waiting to climb onto a shrine, under blue-white streaks of this new moon's hair.

Pingmei Lan grew up in Beijing, China. She received her MFA in creative writing from Pacific University in 2018. Her work appears in *Epiphany*, *Tahoma Literary Review*, *Crab Orchard Review*, and other publications. She lives in San Diego.

EDITORS' NOTE

To try and slow the joyously unending flood of stories that come in for consideration at *Lady Churchill's Rosebud Wristlet*, we ask that all submissions come in on paper. This way my coeditor, Kelly Link, and I can keep up. I carry canvas bags of stories home and we read each story in the interstices of publishing and home life. From those sacks and stacks, only a few stories will fit our tastes—which is why for writers it is so useful to read a range of magazines to find where to send their stories. Many of those stories will find other editors who are looking for different stories.

A. B. Young's "Vain Beasts" stood out immediately. When I open those envelopes, discard the cover letter so that I can approximate the reader's reading experience, and read, I am always hoping for a story such as this, where the writer takes the threads of story and weaves something new. Here is a writer who knows the rules of fairy tales, who plays with time and structure and familiar characters and ideas and makes something unique; who approaches the mysterious yet never leaves the reader ungrounded. This story, with its circles and repetitions, is a rich deep dive into the choices people make in their lives, and the costs and burdens borne by ourselves and others.

Gavin J. Grant and Kelly Link, Publishers
Lady Churchill's Rosebud Wristlet

VAIN BEASTS

A. B. Young

The unheard-breach of faith not
Feigned feeling to fill other vacancies
—Gloria Frym, *Mind Over Matter*

DORIAN GRAY FORGETS to pray most nights, listening instead to
the cat caw on the back porch; listening with the cat for the crows
to caw back. Wind whispers to the tired plaster walls, and sweat
drips from the roof to the carpet of browning roses.

DORIAN GRAY CROSSES the village square on shoes that click as
they lift from the cobblestones. The seamstress and her beau, with
fingers curled around the edges of each other's pockets, pause to
watch him pass but don't notice that the footsteps sound out of
time. They look, instead, at the mask he wears beneath his hooded
cloak. It is the taxidermied face of a fog-white wolf, fangs bared,
eye cavities excavated. He walks with long, sure strides in the fading light.

He speaks to no one, but does turn to look at those who stop
to watch him. The wolf mask sits slightly crooked on his face, and

the long snout tilts, as if the wolf's head is cocked. Murk glares out from where eyes should be.

When he reaches the edge of the woods, he follows a hard, worn path through the trees and to the grove of the moon goddess. An altar sits beside a shallow pool, and on it black roses float in a bowl of water.

He stops walking at the edge of the pool. The sound of his clacking footsteps continues for several seconds after.

He waits, silent, still. He waits for six minutes.

"Your vanity makes you patient," a woman's voice says from behind him. He starts just slightly, his intestines pressing up and out against his ribs. Then he feels a palm pressed flat on his back before the fingers curl to grope his cloak. "And you smell of blue salts. Of neem," the voice continues, moving closer to his ear, carried on warm breath. "How odd you are, Dorian Gray."

"You smell of cinnamon and coal," he replies, because she does. He stays very still.

The hand moves, cloak still clutched in fingers, across his side. Around to his front. She splays her palm across his belly. His shirt is thin linen, but he can feel no warmth at all from her skin.

"You have a request for me, Dorian Gray. Speak it."

There is a moment of quiet and her order lingers. Something smells vaguely of burning.

"Beauty," he whispers, and her hand presses more firmly into his gut.

"Tell me, Dorian Gray," she says, and her voice is scattered flour, settling into crevices. "Are you afraid of wolves?"

"No," he replies.

She says, "One day you will be."

———

CALLUSES CAPTURE SPLINTERS as the woodcutter handles his kindling. His hands are deft, like pliable bark; firm, but flaking. The blanket of felt is spread on the dirt and the leaves, and it's green in the light of his lamp, black in the light of the moon. He bends at the waist, gathers firewood to his chest, and turns to place it on the blanket. He grunts with the effort of straightening. He rolls his neck. The sweat slinks down, and the pain in his strained muscles scrapes up.

It is this night, as he trudges home, that he meets the fairy. She opens her arms, opens. She says, *You are tired, let me hold your axe.* Her voice is melting snowflakes on the tips of his ears. The woodcutter wears boots lined with deerskin and a coat of stiff green linen, his beard perfectly trimmed to the shape of his chin. He opens the blanket and lets the cut wood shatter on the dirt. The blanket falls to the ground like a dead leaf.

She opens her arms, clothed by moonlight and not clothed at all.

Their bodies fill to the threshold with splinters.

THE FIRST NIGHT he is missing, the woodcutter's wife lets her stew solidify to slush. The table smells of roses, pine, and cinnamon. She sits, back pressed straight, with the two wooden bowls, the two copper spoons, the firelight joyous and dying. Her deerskin shawl mutters to her cheek. The base of her back whimpers.

His wife waits for him for a decade. When she marries again, her dress is cumbersome and cream.

———

THERE ARE MANY nights that the woodcutter does not meet the fairy. There are also many nights that he does, and never returns.

Only one night does he get lost on his way home.

The full moon drapes its light over Dorian Gray's shutters, crawling like a rejected lover across his pine dining table, across his face. His cheekbones are set low, jutting against skin covered in crusted craters. His wolf mask hangs by the front door, and his metal-heeled shoes sit atop the stove. His cloak is on the floor beside his bed. He sits slumped in a hard wooden chair beside the table. He holds a small mirror in his pale hands, and watches, waiting. He sits very still. Then he hears a tapping at his door.

THE FRIAR COUNTS the witches who've been sacrificed to the devil. The devil counts his teeth.

There's a tapping at the friar's door, and at first he thinks it is the branch of a tree. He sits in his favorite chair, the one that closes around him like lips. He has lived here for years, in a house beside the grove at the base of the stream. There he built an altar, protected by a waystone. He tends to the altar nightly, leaving black roses for the moon.

JULIET IS PICKING flowers in a field when her father comes home. She picks only the white ones, breaking the stems close to the dirt. She intends to take them home and weave crowns for her sisters. The crowns will die tomorrow and the three girls will sigh in sadness, their breath blowing like a gale over shriveled petals. But Juliet does not think of that now, singing to the deerskin shawl that razes her cheeks.

Her father calls to her from the barn.

Her bare feet murmur to the soft spring soil as she lifts her dirt-smeared skirt and races the breeze. Her father stands at the door, tall as a cliff-face, axe over his left shoulder.

He says, "Come, Juliet. I have brought you a gift from my travels."

She asks, "Have you brought me a rose?"

It is all she had asked for.

He replies, "Yes, my beauty," and produces a black rose to add to her armful of daisies.

ON THE NIGHT he gets lost the woodcutter is caught unprepared by the speed of nightfall. He realizes he has gone too far in the wrong direction, but he can't remember the way he came.

He wanders until he comes to the cottage of Dorian Gray. Except, this night, the cottage is a castle. The stone towers cast shadows for a mile, thin and straight, like pine trees stripped of their branches.

When the woodcutter comes to the gate he places a hand on the rusted metal, and the grimy cold of it bites into his palm. The cobblestone path is covered in dirt, gray moss sprouting between its cracks. The high hedges bordering the path, however, are pristine, rustling in the breeze. Moon-white flowers bloom among the dark green.

The woodcutter follows the path, ignoring the prickling at the back of his neck, ignoring how the chill in his palm creeps up his forearm. He hears the crunch of the dirt under his feet. His footsteps echo strangely, and it's as if he can feel them in his jaw, out of time.

"Hello?" the woodcutter calls, but the word is instantly gobbled up by the wind.

He notices the stone gargoyles peering down from the tower roofs. They mark his procession through the garden, and the wood-cutter imagines that if he could get closer to their faces he would see the eyes were only excavated cavities, and their snouts were howling like wolves.

The woodcutter sees the wall of a tower where roses climb. The roses are black, their velvet petals shimmering in the moonlight. They nestle among thorns that are long and curved like fingernails. He moves toward the wall, drawn to it. Enchanted. He reaches out a hand and presses it to a rose. He presses until he feels the thorns digging into his skin. He presses until they break his skin, until the rose petals are crushed and smeared with blood in his palm. The cold crawls farther up his arm, nearing his shoulder.

He withdraws, thorns embedded in his skin.

A voice behind him demands, "What have you done?"

BLACK ROSES SHRIVEL with brown, drift on brown water, en-snared in brown bowl.

There's a tapping at the friar's door, and at first he thinks it is the branch of a tree. He sits in his warmest chair, the one that closes around him like a curling tongue. His knees shudder as he clambers to his feet. In a nightgown of felt, he shuffles and creaks to the door.

He grasps the oyster-shell knob; its edges nibble his palm. He opens the door and the leaves of the trees applaud. The smiling flames in the hearth make the room glow gold, and when he opens the door, her hands look copper.

———

THE WOODCUTTER'S BLANKET is made of felt and the leaves and
twigs come closer to feel the static, then stay. He wraps his firewood, and the bundle could contain an adolescent girl, all uneven
limbs. He clutches it to his chest.

It is this night, as he trudges home, that he meets the fairy. She
wears a deerskin shawl. Her silver hair floats on the heavy air, and
she says, *You are tired, let me hold your axe.*

But he's left his axe among the tree stumps.

DORIAN GRAY HAS roses on his dining table. His cottage smells of
cinnamon and pine. He was beautiful once; he remembers this. He
looks into a shard of glass and sees pale hair, thin eyelids, mouth
plucked at the edges of naivety.

His wife sings outside, by the window, voice tumbling in with
the sunlight as she tends to the roses. She sings to the sun of the
moon's envy.

The cottage is all brown and gray. Wooden rushes on the floor,
ashes in the hearth. Dorian Gray sits at his dining room table and
listens to his wife sing and the cat mumble to itself on the windowsill. The moments pass like cricket croaks and finally he shouts,
"Oh, fair sun!"

Juliet stops singing.

ON THE NIGHT the woodcutter meets Dorian Gray, he meets not a
man, but a wolf. A voice says, "What have you done?"

In fright, the woodcutter presses the thorn of the rose farther into his finger. He turns to see the fog-white wolf, eyes scarred and black. "I'm lost," he replies, his voice small and glassy.

"Do all lost men steal other men's flowers?" asks the wolf.

The woodcutter stutters. "You are not a man."

The wolf cocks his head and barks a laugh. His breath smells of blue salts and neem. He says, "Tell me, woodcutter, are you afraid of wolves?"

THE WOODCUTTER IS indeed afraid of wolves. He tells the fairy this, as he watches her chop firewood. She places a log on the stump then nudges it to the center with her mud-covered foot. Her temporal thigh pulls downwards, pulsing away from her bones in waves. The woodcutter says, "The wolves will come if we don't leave soon. Oughtn't you go home?" He brushes his nails against his bollocks, looking around for his linen jacket.

The fairy says nothing, removing her foot from the stump. She raises the axe, both hands tight at the edge of the handle, and she flings it back over her head so her whole body must follow its procession. She balances on her toes, her body the waning crescent moon.

In the distance, a crow caws, and a wolf whimpers back. The pressure of the axe blade splits the log and it crackles.

THE GROVE BESIDE the friar's house shudders like dragonfly wings. The waystone flicks shadows over the base of the stream, wind fingering the water until it shimmers.

There's a tapping at the friar's door, and this time he thinks it is the devil come for kindling.

———

DORIAN GRAY LOOKS up at the moon through the dark green leaves. He savors the scream in the base of his back and how it scrambles, all splintering nails, up, hollowing the muscles either side of his spine, to clench his shoulders. He feels the muscles pulled taut as bones try to escape his skin, pushing like the foot of a baby against the walls of his mother's womb. He is warmed by the fur that breaks through his skin like goosepimples. The cracking of bones is drowned out by pants and howls. He listens, hoping to hear the caws of crows.

THE FAIRY TELLS Dorian Gray, *I will trade you the greatest of pleasures for your beauty.* He licks his lips. His eyes follow the fall of her black hair, hung heavy to touch the moss and tickle her ankles. He asks, "Are you afraid of wolves?"

Her lips turn up into the waxing crescent moon.

JULIET PULLS THE deerskin shawl tighter. Her breath, mist before her face, clears away to reveal looming towers and murky turrets that were not there moments before.

"Tell me, Juliet," says her father, "are you afraid of wolves?"

HER BACK GOES cold like there's water seeping up, under her skin. Dorian Gray is very close behind her. If he were to put a hand on her, the heat would sear through her dress. His chin mists along her neck, and with lips at her ear, he says, "Juliet, you are beauty." She swallows and the saliva won't pass the stone she feels in her throat. It bubbles back up and she gags. His hand hits her flat in the center of her back. Her diaphragm seizes, her shoulders shudder forward, and the burp races up, spherical slime, through her chest and carries drool out and down her chin.

Dorian Gray's laugh is like a bark, and it reverberates in her chest.

THE WOLF TELLS the woodcutter, "In exchange for stealing my rose, you will bring me your most beautiful possession."

The woodcutter trembles. He wishes he had not left his axe back among the tree stumps. He could split the wolf into equal halves, had he enough force behind his swing.

The wolf says, "My vanity makes me patient, woodcutter. I have waited many years for beauty."

The woodcutter lies through his sharp teeth. "I have no beautiful possessions. I am a poor woodcutter."

"What?" says the wolf. "No wife? No daughter?"

THE FIRST TIME Dorian Gray asks Juliet to marry him, she looks at his cratered skin, firm but flaking, and she says no. The next day when he proposes again, he wears his wolf mask, and watches her through the excavated eyes as she rejects him again.

On the twentieth day, he pushes her up against his cottage wall, an arm crushed to her throat, and she spits her "no," saliva filled with brown-blood hate, into his face.

Between the fortieth and sixtieth proposal, Dorian Gray falls in love. He cooks for Juliet, venison and goat-milk cheesecakes and stews that fill her with temporal heat. He presses rose-petal kisses to her hands, warm fingers into her palm.

On the seventy-third day, Juliet says yes.

Her beauty becomes his.

THE FIRST TIME he comes home with blood on his lips, Juliet seeks a reasonable explanation. She whispers to the cat that he would never hurt them. After all, he loves her.

THE FRIAR SAYS, "Juliet, I thought you were the moon goddess come to collect my soul." Then he sees the blood on her hands. He sees it smeared across her pale lips. She breathes through her mouth; her warm breath grazes his cheek and smells of cinnamon and burning. There is a tingling beneath his scalp. He says, "My dear, what has happened?"

She says, "I killed the woodcutter. He was a wolf all along."

The friar barks a laugh, and splutters hot spittle onto her cheek.

ON THE NIGHT of her second wedding, the woodcutter's wife goes into the woods. She wears a deerskin shawl over her wedding dress, which is not white. She chops wood for hours, feeling sweat chill against her skin.

It is this night that she meets the fairy.

She is naked as the moon, a slender sliver. Her hair floats on the humid air. She says, *You are tired, let me hold your axe.*

Juliet is indeed tired, she is not often up so late. She holds the axe out, head down, and watches as the translucent fingers of the fairy grasp it. She notices rough divots in the skin, like craters. The silver blade glints in the moonlight as the fairy lifts it over her head. She swings it forward to meet with Juliet's white rose crown. The axe splinters bones, slow with shyness, as flesh and golden hair quiver away from the blade. Black guts splatter fairy feet. Juliet tumbles to both sides as separate halves.

DORIAN GRAY LIES in bed and ponders the fickleness of women. The strangled screech of a crow that cawed back to the cat seeps in with the wind through the sweltering walls. The cat's tail quivers.

———————————

A. B. Young learned to tell stories from playing with Barbies. She learned to tell stories well at California College of the Arts. She now teaches kids how to read stories and write essays about them as a high school media and English teacher.

EDITOR'S NOTE

When Erin Singer's manuscript arrived out of the blue at our office, we were floored by the originality of her voice. The complicated but always moving family portrait that emerges against its backdrop of hardscrabble life in Saskatchewan offers unexpected insights into a life seldom depicted in prose. Singer shows familial love manifesting itself in hauntingly different ways, and she manages to capture the all-too-common struggles and affections of a fractured household in a unique setting, while subverting conventional expectations of female narratives. With memorable nuance and diamond-sharp wit, "Bad Northern Women" reads like the work of a seasoned writer, one possessed of vivid wisdom beyond her years.

Bradford Morrow, Editor
Conjunctions

BAD NORTHERN WOMEN

Erin Singer

WE ARE TOCKERS, descendants of thirty-six feet of long lean Saskatchewan woman: six Tocker sisters, six foot tall, exemplary ax-women all, so says our mom. At the kitchen table this morning we are mixing our Nesquik and Mom is quoting from *Taking Our Time: A History of Tockers*. As she cites each Tocker triumph she stabs the book with her file, showering its curling cover with fingernail dust. Tocker Trucking! Compass Sawmill! TT's Laundromat! Stab! Stab! Stab! Mom plants the file in an old baby corn can crammed with white pencil crayons and shards of rulers and dried-out pens. She rubs her eyes until mascara moons arise underneath. Our spoons clack inside our plastic cups.

What was I saying? She sighs. Point being, summer's coming and no Tocker ever chopped a tree indoors. Get outside and play! Tocker girls brown up good. Just godsakes don't get a farmer tan.

That right there's offensive to farmers, Dad says behind his cigarette smoke.

I'm going down for a nap, says Mom. She puts her Kool-Aid glass in the sink.

Dad lifts his chin to the nip marks on our legs.

What's this? He bends, grabs our pup by the snout for a one-on-one: You're supposed to scare them feral beasts off.

Mom says, If these girls can't handle a couple of strays, how will they learn to handle a man?

Dad's not worried about that. Because! he says. *Because* I got a feeling this one's going to shape up to be a good guard dog.

Mom snorts, says, I like my animals wild and in my tummy.

The dog is a freebie from Swap 'N' Shop. He's a weird-looking guy, kind of a fluffy coyote. Dad claims his name is Chopper but we're not convinced.

Don't fail me now, he warns the pup. Can't watch my girls every minute. More like any minute. Dad spends his days under the Chev Suburban he's liberating from our driveway. He's getting itchy. Threatening to head north this time.

He follows Mom down the hall to her bedroom. Go play, he says.

Teenage girls don't play. So we walk. We walk Airport Road until there's the hum of an approaching plane. Checking over our shoulders, we break into a run. The airplane descends from the south, twin propellers whirring over great squares of green spring prairie, silver circles of grain bins and farmhouse roofs streaked rusty with wood-smoke. It lands short of the darkness of white spruce and jack pine gathered on the horizon. We are close enough that we can see the white blobs of strange faces in the dark windows as the plane shoots by us, blowing past the warning signs. CAUTION! STRAY DOGS ON THE RUNWAY!

American bear hunters in khaki and camo step onto the tarmac. There is only one dog in sight and he belongs to us: four stringy teenage girls in ribbed tank tops and basketball shorts pressed against the chain-link fence. The hunters are too far away to see our winter-pale legs knotted with mosquito bites, our gnawed fingernails, our silver-filled molars, our greasy hair Mom chopped short as punishment for, as she puts it, not learning to work a shampoo bottle.

The hunters laugh at something we can't hear, which is the pilot saying, Welcome to the North, where the men are men and the women are too.

The ditch is dry and we follow it along Highway 4. The pup leaps and runs in circles and stops to sniff a squashed porcupine. Foxtails grow along the road and we tear them from the ground and brush the silk across our lips. We hurdle over fully loaded baby diapers and broken beer bottles as we go north to Bart's Gas.

The Gladue girls have the picnic table. They are cracking and firing off dill pickle Spitz shells to the dirt below. These chicks are Cree and they glow. They've got that sunny maple-syrup skin that we can't get no matter how many hours Mom forces us out in the sun. The Gladue girls are named for old movie stars.

Too much grease in that hair, *moonyasses*, says Whoopi, scratching our pup's tawny fur. Your bangs look like string cheese.

The boys say your panties smell like muskeg.

Puckamahow, says Daryl. Then she puts up two fists and laughs at our chickenshit eyes.

Let's go, then.

As if.

Too dumb you are. Look in the mirror.

Bored, we leave. There is nowhere new to walk. Tocker Town has no surprises, no hidden staircases, no haunted conservatories, no secret garden. We know this place like the inside of our parents' underwear drawers. Today is Saturday. No school. No money. No jobs yet but summer is coming. Work will claim us. Crappy jobs come like power poles on the highway.

Before we die we'll slick your Teen Burgers with Teen Sauce,

make chicken salad on a cheese bun and keep your kids from
drowning in the public pool and we are jolly bun fillers of subma-
rine sandwiches and we ring up your Trojans and Lysol and scented
candles, and we shovel your snow and push your babies on the
swing set, pare your grandpa's toenails, harvest your honey, detail
your urinals, hold the papery hands of your dying, nestle newspapers in the rungs of your mailbox and ladle gravy on your French
fries and we push logs through your sawmill, bring you size-ten
Sorels, then size eleven, then size ten and a half, and climb onto our
mattresses at night with gasoline on our hands and dog bites on our
ankles, chicken fingers on our breath, cigarette smoke in our hair,
ringing in our ears and our men's hands snaking up our thighs.

With nowhere to go we walk home, which is the most mysterious place of all. We take turns carrying the pup because the stray
dog pack starts shadowing us when we cut through the Video
Express parking lot.

At home Mom is up from her nap and planting the garden, tan-
ning off her wrinkles in a slack Value Village bikini. There's dirt on
her knees, goose bumps on the loose flesh of her thighs.

She says, I'm standing in the graveyard of my summer.

Mom tells us we aren't allowed inside unless we plan to shower,
because we look like we've dipped our heads in an outhouse hole.

From underneath the Suburban, Dad says, I've known your
mom to camp in the bush for a week and come out smelling fresher
than the day she went in.

He lays it on superthick with Mom when he's itching. Might
very well be up and gone soon as the Suburban is humming. He
used to say he couldn't bear his women for more than a season but
he's been here all year.

Yeah right. How's that?

How? How, they want to know? Mom stabs her Garden Claw in the ground. Hoo, boy! Nobody ever told *me*. Nobody taught *me* a damn thing. Look how I turned out.

You're perfect, Mother, calls Dad.

Mom scowls.

Dad claims the Tocker Town job market is a dust bowl. There hasn't been so-called real man's work since he returned from whatever boomtown venture or hunting extravaganza he left us for last time.

Lately he's telling us how we couldn't imagine what all connections he's got in the Yukon. The Yukon is the *true* true north strong and free of which we sing at school every morning and before minor hockey games of boys who call us hatchet faces (which, at first, we think is because of the Tockers' work in the forestry industry).

Dad crabwalks out from under the Suburban, arms skinny as a new carrot. He climbs in the driver's seat and smiles through the windshield at nothing. He's just sitting there like a toddler in a plastic car on the lawn.

Mom says, Tockers who leave aren't real Tockers at all.

Fine, Dad says, staring, that faraway smile on his lips. I'm gonna drive to Whitehorse and when I get there I'm gonna order pizza every day and the pizza will always be meat lovers'.

Our stomachs sing dirges.

Even if Mom won't go?

Even if Mom won't go.

Even if we don't go?

Well, I can't spank you no more so is there anything specific I can do for you?

Tell us we're pretty.

My girls are the prettiest girls north of North Battleford and south of sixty and half my heart will pretty near disappear if you don't come along. Man's gotta keep his family together.

He can sweet-talk with impunity because he knows Mom is a mountain. Where she is, we are. Even awful mothers are everything.

Mom, let's all go this time. For real. C'mon. Let's go.

In her garden, Mom levels Dad with eyes black as old bear scat. I'm due to get drawn for moose this fall, she says. I'll drop all you like a cigarette butt before I give up my Saskatchewan hunting license.

We watch her tearing the earth with her claw.

Thing is, girls, man needs his woman to have a little mystery to her, Dad says. But don't overdo it.

The whole trailer is damp with the steam of four showers. We sit on the floor of the living room while Mom stretches over the couch, dozing in and out with a glass of cherry Kool-Aid balanced on her gut. She's pulled on an old Oilers shirt. Her bikini top is collapsed on the carpet beside us. We watch what's on the CBC because we don't have a dish and we don't need one anyway. The news says two teenagers got shot in a shopping-mall food court in Guelph.

No food courts here, murmurs Mom, eyes half-closed with a gassy newborn smile.

The Saturday movie is about the queen of our hearts, Princess Diana. She's pregnant and falls down a flight of stairs.

Dad comes in wiping grease on his jeans. No stairs in a trailer, he says. Youse guys got it better than Lady Di.

No one laughs. Humbled, he wonders, Will there be supper to-night, Mother?

Mom shrugs. I'm going to take a hot bath. See if that'll knock me out.

She likes to keep us guessing, keep us hungry. Hunger might be better than what she offers. She cooks with passive aggression. I am mad at you, says the elk liver and onions. Don't be a pussy, says the bear-and-turnip stew. Her Swiss beaver steak says, I'll make you bad northern women.

Who is a bad northern woman?

She is the opposite of a good southern girl.

Mom's supper could make you whimper for hamburgers that taste like cow and sausages that taste like pig. Pop the lid on our deep freeze and marvel at our foggy bagged bread, our icy peas, our pile of wild meat. Whether you can stomach it or not, there is always food. Later, when we're grown, Mom will fall back on this: I never let you go hungry, she says again and again.

Eat, she'll goad from the head of the table. Puts hair on your chest like fish hooks.

And Dad will say, Damn rights, I wouldn't go chest to chest with my old lady.

After you eat, make yourself scarce. You don't really like it here and we don't want you anyway.

This is our northern hospitality.

We press our ears to the door as the bathwater runs. On the other side Dad is telling Mom that the Suburban's engine turned over this morning. He implores her to imagine the true northern delicacies a Yukon stove could yield: giant boiled moose head, Dall sheep shanks rank with game, caribou barbecue.

Mom says, Yeah, but do they have Tockers there?

No, he says, they have trees. The Yukon is full of trees waiting to fall.

If he wants her to come that means he wants us, too.

You dough head, says Mom. Strong trees grow here. The ones up north are weak.

I never heard that, says Dad. You don't know that.

Mom's voice softens. Now stop it. You're not going anywhere. Come here.

Sometimes we can tell the difference between the sounds of our parents' love and the sounds of their anger. Both horrify. We depart.

The Lions Park playground is empty. Someone has taken all the swings and looped them around the wooden frame out of reach. There are tractor tires painted primary colors humping out of the grass and we climb the giant treads, pull up the hems of our shorts and tank tops, and swing our legs in the sun.

There's the usual talk about our future truck. The specific model is yet to be settled but of course not a Ford. The color will be pure white. The air freshener will be mango. The tires will be as enormous as the ones underneath us. Big enough to cruise around town looking down on everyone else's roof. There's nothing mysterious about a girl in a shitty car.

Then there's tough talk about how if Dad goes again, he's dead to us. Half of us think he really wants us to come. Mom has dared us to say yes to him. See our invitation evaporate, she says.

Our stomachs creak and groan. At first we laugh and poke our bellies. Then we grow restless, suddenly sick to death of each other, seeing everything we hate about ourselves on each other's dumb faces. We kick the tires, flick our lighters, and push their tops into the rubber until it melts. Without speaking we walk back to Bart's Gas to try to stir up something. This time only Daryl is on the picnic table, letting Peps Derocher lick Cheezie dust from her finger. She rolls her eyes and sends a half-hearted kick of dirt our way.

Not now.

We walk up one side of Tocker Town Main Street and down the other. We go in the hobby shop and loiter in the aisles just to bug the cashier who always accuses us of stealing. We go in the grocery store and we steal a box of Glosette peanuts and a mango.

The pup follows us to the highway, where we race beer cans off the side of Jonas Tocker Memorial Bridge, so named for a great-uncle who got drunk, crashed his car, and burned down the original. (*Taking Our Time* tells the story a little different.) We stick our thumbs out to hitch. Logging trucks blow by and lift the hair from our scalps. No one stops. It was a joke anyway.

Over by the swimming pool the stray dog pack circles us and licks our legs. Before we can grab the pup, a mangy collie with a cloudy eye nips him. We holler and take turns carrying our little boy. A block from home, we bowl the mango down a culvert. That's when we hear the thunderous roaring, a belligerent engine revved to life. Our father whooping, his voice a gold rush.

Supper is stringy wild goose, salt-and-pepper-roasted with a freezer-burn finish. Dad feels his shirt pocket for a smoke before he even sets his fork down, that's how quick he needs the taste out of his mouth. Mom licks her purpled lips, one paw curled around luminous juice. She wants to know if we've heard her very own tale of the drowning eagle.

Many times.

When I was about your age, I knew this eagle that come to nest every year by Tocker Lake, Mom begins. I'd go there to swim or just lie alone for hours until my skin was brown as a marshmallow on a wiener stick. One afternoon, I felt our eagle passing over. Sure enough, she was swooping down to the water for some grub. Oh, what a beauty. So powerful she could hook the thickest walleye in the drink. Seen her a million times but each time was like the first. Now, that afternoon, this eagle's feet go up and she spreads her curly talons for lunch but it's not until she's got those claws sunk in good that she realizes she's hooked onto a big old jackfish.

Mom sips her Kool-Aid. She leans into us.

Now, I got a look at the hoary bastard. I got a flash of that big, meaty water rat in her talons as she tried to lift it and, oh, this poor bitch is struggling. She's trying to fly back up in the air where she belongs and the jack just keeps dragging her down. She fights good but it's no use. He sank her. The eagle drowned. Dead.

Mom slaps her hand on the table. The cutlery jumps. At least she died at home, she says to Dad.

After supper we go out the bedroom window. Climb and pull each other to the roof to eat dry ice cream cones because our stomachs are burning. The pup yelps from the bedroom where we've trapped him. After nine and the sun is finally fading. Mom is working her night shift at the old folks' home, a place where she claims to eat shit forty hours a week. This is Mom's only story that never rings true.

Below our dangling feet, Dad ferries rifle cases and toolboxes and garbage bags of clothes from the trailer to the Suburban. After tonight his underwear drawer is nothing but pennies and rolling bullet casings. The sky is fairy-tale blue, lit by gold, fixed up with fleecy white clouds. We talk about Princess Diana, how sad her life was. How if she'd had a big truck, well, she'd still be alive. We agree she would've liked us. At bedtime we discover the pup has peed on the bedroom carpet. We fall asleep without cleaning it up.

In the morning Dad gives us one final pitch. He asks us who we want to be.

We want to be this one chick at school, the setter on the volley-ball team who buys all her clothes in the city.

Dad shakes his head, frowning. No, he says, we can pick any-one, anywhere. Like cast fishing lures we can sparkle and soar. We are tethered only when our line hits the light.

But that chick lives here.

Maybe, says Dad, maybe up north all youse will be that chick. Up there who will know your names?

Exactly!

Dad surrenders, palms in the air. The record shows: he tried.

Mom sprays her planters with a garden hose.

Do I need to check my purse? she says. Did you clean me out again?

She's still dressed in her scrubs because she hasn't gone to bed yet. She fans the hose over her poppy patch. We hug Dad goodbye. Does he really think we'll come? Nope, he tells us later. You're your mother's daughters.

Maybe so, but we aren't Tockers. Mom isn't either, not re-ally. Before Mom married Dad she was an Ekert. Her grandma, Grandma Olga, was one of those behemoth Tocker sisters, but Great-Grandma Olga's mother, the lady who pumped out those thirty-six feet of long lean Saskatchewan woman, she was some other name that nobody committed to memory or bothered writ-ing down because she didn't have a self-published family fairy-tale book.

Dad comes up behind Mom and says, Anything good that's go-ing to happen to me here's already happened.

Who's waiting for something good to happen? Mom says.

Pfft, Dad huffs. He gets in the Suburban and says, Probably bet-ter this way, eh?

He backs out and away with morning light passing through the empty windows.

What'd I tell you, says Mom, turning to us, red-eyed and jowly jawed.

The hose hisses as Mom crushes some peonies with water. The pup scrabbles out of our grip and gives chase. We look from the dog to Mom.

Good riddance, she says and turns the hose on herself. The spray plasters her thin hair to her forehead and cheeks, water streaming down her face, dripping from her chin. She yells at us to shut up.

Running through dust kicked up by Dad's wheels we chase after Chopper. Chopper is speedy. The little guy is nowhere in sight so we run for Highway 4, the only way north. Sure enough, the pup is trotting down the centerline. A car swerves and honks and Chopper ambles to the ditch. Drops out of view. At the junction of Highway 4 and Railway Avenue a van with Manitoba plates pulls alongside us and honks. We're watching cars, timing a dart across. The man in the van says, You girls are gorgeous. He laughs and spittle flies out the space where his front teeth should be. He revs an engine so old it sounds like Dad at the sink in the morning, sputtering, growling, unearthing treasures from his smoker's chest.

This man yells over the engine, She runs dirty but she can go!

There is a truck barreling toward us as we dash across. White line, yellow lines, white line, ditch. Chopper is trotting through the new spring grass, sniffing some dog crap by the service road. We call to him but he doesn't know his name.

The dog pack crests the approach in front of the Chinese restaurant. There are four of them today: the collie, a sick terrier, a gray pit bull, a white shepherd with a speckled face. Chopper goes right to the pack, yipping at the bigger dogs. The collie snaps at him. We scream. The dogs growl and bark. Chopper darts to us but the collie catches him at the neck.

Frozen-eyed, Chopper flops side to side, a wild noodle in the dog's mouth. His fluffy coyote tail sweeps the grass. We leap into the pack and grab the collie by the hindquarters and yank them like a wishbone and pound his body with our fists. Chopper falls to the ground and we scoop him up. Our screams are high and shrill. The pit bull leaps at our legs, tearing at our skin. A truck rips in off the highway and a door slams and in the golden eastern morning light filtering through the dust, there is our father. Hear his sweet holler.

We run as he boots the collie. He grabs the terrier by the scruff of his neck and tosses him. Dogs yelp and scatter. The animals speed off into the fallow field beyond the Chinese restaurant.

Dad drives us home. Says he could hear our screams from Bart's Gas. Chopper whines. The fur on his neck is bloody but he licks our wounds.

Seems like you'll be okay, right, boy? Dad says to the pup.

All these years off and on with Mom and still he never learned how to lie.

Mom emerges from her bedroom in a Garfield nightshirt with her damp hair mushed to one side of her face. She smiles, so triumphant at the sight of Dad she doesn't notice our bloody legs, the tear trails on our dusty cheeks.

Seems like there's nothing the five of you despise more than seeing me get a moment's rest, she says.

In our room, hands atremble, we pull T-shirts and stuffed animals and loose tampons out of drawers, forgetting dog food and winter jackets and our last name. Down the hall Dad tells Mom to pack up. Her yell could send a thousand geese back south. Then, silence. Dragging our garbage bags down the hall we stop to rattle the doorknob.

C'mon, Mom, we say, pressing our bodies against her hollow door. She's up against the other side, on the ground, crouched at our feet.

We tell her that even if these strays run off, a new dog blur of mange and eye gunk and broken teeth will appear. We confess we're scared of summer. Every day of our lives will be work and if it's not work, every day will be like today.

Worse, she laughs. It gets so much worse.

First Dad drives to Bart's so he can finish gassing up. The Gladue girls are at the picnic table. We get out.

Dogs got you, eh, says Whoopi. She reaches over and scratches the sharp bridge of Chopper's nose. Hey, she says, ever think he looks like a coyote?

We tell the Gladue girls we are going to the Yukon.

For vacation?

No. Forever.

But school's not done yet.

We ask them if they know about the eagle that got drowned by the jackfish.

Where'd you hear that?

Our mom.

They laugh.

Your people could win medals for bullshit, says Whoopi.

Eagles don't drown, dummies, says Daryl. You can't believe how good eagles swim.

Dad comes back from paying. He thumps a hand on the roof. Say bye to your friends, ladies. Consider us long gone.

When he slides into the driver's seat, he grips the wheel with both hands and squeezes. Usually we fight to ride shotgun. The four of us climb in the back.

Well, bye then, Whoopi says through the open window.

Bon voyage, offers Daryl. To maintain equilibrium, she licks her finger and draws a quick cock and balls in the dust clinging to the Suburban. At a gas station outside Fort Nelson, as Dad rants about how much girls have to stop to pee, we'll see her drawing and feel sadness that we won't yet identify as homesickness.

Bye, we call to the Gladue girls.

The girls return to the picnic table. Gravel crunches and pops under our slow tires. The feathers of a dollar-store dream catcher on our rearview mirror flutter as the Suburban gains speed. Dad rolls up our windows and stills our dancing hair.

He says, Jesus Murphy, girls, look at your old dad now. He takes off his ball cap, tosses it on the passenger seat. Rubs his bald spot. Lights a cigarette. He says, You know it won't be no cakewalk in the Yukon. You girls are going to have to buckle down. Help me out till Mom gets there.

The highway roars. Two kilometers out, we zoom past a reflective green sign welcoming visitors to our town: MUSKA LAKE: YOUR GATEWAY TO THE NORTH.

Dad drives north and west. The bones of our knees press together. The pup shakes on our laps, claws stabbing through the nylon of our shorts.

Our blood dries as Dad drives. We trace our fingers over the marks on our long Tocker limbs. In the years to come, many more apart than we ever were together, we never stop telling our childhood. We remember the white trails of each other's scars like they are our own.

Inside the Suburban, we leave tractors dragging seeders, men toppling jack pine, and our mother lying on a mangy bedroom carpet, waiting. We don't turn back. We are four strays strung by seat belts, fingers against a windowpane as bush and bears and burning cigarettes whiz by.

———————

Erin Singer grew up in the Yukon and northwest Saskatchewan. She lives in Las Vegas.

ABOUT THE JUDGES

DANIELLE EVANS is the author of *Before You Suffocate Your Own Fool Self*, which was a co-winner of the 2011 PEN/Robert W. Bingham Prize for a Debut Short Story Collection, the winner of the 2011 Paterson Fiction Prize and the 2011 Hurston/Wright Legacy Award for fiction, and an honorable mention for the 2011 PEN/Hemingway Award. She teaches in The Writing Seminars at Johns Hopkins University.

ALICE SOLA KIM is a winner of the 2016 Whiting Award. Her writing has appeared or is forthcoming in *Tin House*, *McSweeney's*, *BuzzFeed*, and *The Year's Best Science Fiction & Fantasy*. She has received grants and scholarships from the MacDowell Colony, Bread Loaf Writers' Conference, and the Elizabeth George Foundation.

CARMEN MARIA MACHADO's debut short story collection, *Her Body and Other Parties*, was a finalist for the National Book Award, the Kirkus Prize, the Art Seidenbaum Award for First Fiction, the World Fantasy Award, the International Dylan Thomas Prize, and the PEN/Robert W. Bingham Prize for a Debut Short Story Collection, and the winner of the Bard Fiction Prize, the Lambda Literary Award for Lesbian Fiction, the Brooklyn Public Library Literary Prize, the Shirley Jackson Award, and the National Book Critics Circle's John Leonard Prize. She is the writer in residence at the University of Pennsylvania.

ABOUT THE PEN/ROBERT J. DAU SHORT STORY PRIZE FOR EMERGING WRITERS

The PEN/Robert J. Dau Short Story Prize for Emerging Writers recognizes twelve fiction writers for a debut short story published in a print or online literary magazine. The annual award was offered for the first time during PEN's 2017 awards cycle.

The twelve winning stories are selected by a committee of three judges. The writers of the stories each receive a $2,000 cash prize and are honored at the annual PEN Literary Awards Ceremony in New York City. Every year, Catapult will publish the winning stories in *PEN America Best Debut Short Stories*.

This award is generously supported by the family of the late Robert J. Dau, whose commitment to the literary arts has made him a fitting namesake for this career-launching prize. Mr. Dau was born and raised in Petoskey, a city in Northern Michigan in close proximity to Walloon Lake, where Ernest Hemingway had spent his summers as a young boy and which serves as the backdrop for Hemingway's *The Torrents of Spring*. Petoskey is also known for being where Hemingway determined that he would commit to becoming a writer. This proximity to literary history ignited the Dau family's interest in promoting emerging voices in fiction and spotlighting the next great fiction writer.

LIST OF PARTICIPATING PUBLICATIONS

PEN America and Catapult gratefully acknowledge the following magazines, which published debut fiction in 2018 and submitted work for consideration to the PEN/Robert J. Dau Short Story Prize.

805 Lit + Art
adda
Adolphus Journal
Alaska Quarterly Review
Anomaly Literary Journal
A Public Space
Atlantic Short Story Competition Anthology
Auburn Avenue
AZURE: A Journal of Literary Thought
The Baltimore Review
The Bare Life Review
Bat City Review
Bazzanella Literary Awards Anthology
Bellevue Literary Review
Bennington Review
Birdy Magazine
Black Warrior Review
Body Without Organs
BOMB Magazine
The Brooklyn Review
Carve
Catamaran
Chicago Quarterly Review
Columbia Journal

The Common

Conjunctions

CRAFT

Crazyhorse

DIAGRAM

Epiphany

Exposition Review

The Florida Review

Fourteen Hills: The SFSU Review

Glimmer Train

Granta

Harvard Review

The Iowa Review

J Journal

Juked

KGB Bar Lit Mag

Kweli Journal

Lady Churchill's Rosebud Wristlet

Levitate

LitMag

Meridian Magazine

Mississippi Review

New England Review

New Ohio Review

Nimrod International Journal

Noble / Gas Qtrly

NOON

Out of the Gutter

Paper Darts

Passages North

Pembroke Magazine

Pigeon Pages

Ploughshares

Quarter After Eight

River Styx

The Rumpus

Scribble

The Sewanee Review

Shenandoah

SLICE

SmokeLong Quarterly

Stone Canoe

StoryQuarterly

Subtropics

The Sun

|tap| lit mag

Timothy McSweeney's Quarterly Concern

Tin House

Virginia Quarterly Review

The Wild Word

Witness

Zoetrope: All-Story

ZYZZYVA

PERMISSIONS

PEN America stands at the intersection of literature and human rights to protect open expression in the United States and worldwide. The organization champions the freedom to write, recognizing the power of the word to transform the world. Its mission is to unite writers and their allies to celebrate creative expression and defend the liberties that make it possible.

PEN.ORG